THE WAVES OF HELSINKI

A Jussi Alonen Thriller

John Swallow

Copyright © 2020 John Swallow

All rights reserved

The characters and events portrayed in this book are fictitious. Any similarity to real persons, living or dead, is coincidental and not intended by the author.

No part of this book may be reproduced, or stored in a retrieval system, or transmitted in any form or by any means, electronic, mechanical, photocopying, recording, or otherwise, without express written permission of the publisher.

ISBN-13: 9798699530878
ISBN-10: 1477123456

Cover design by: Art Painter
Library of Congress Control Number: 2018675309
Printed in the United States of America

CONTENTS

Title Page	
Copyright	
In Helsinki	1
The Harbour	16
Found Adrift	27
Date Night	34
The Island	39
The Photograph	52
Disappearing Act	60
Shots Fired	66
In Riga	76
Midsummer Night	94
Lucky Break	104
Narrow Escape	111
The Snitch	121
To Mariehamn	129
The Hideout	143
Saint Petersburg	154
The Fugitive	173
Diplomatic Relations	184
Desperate Measures	191

Frontal Assault	195
Dodging Bullets	204
Close Shave	216
In Rauma	223
About The Author	227
The Jussi Alonen Detective Adventures	229

IN HELSINKI

It was one of those never-ending summer days. The sky was bright turquoise, and the sunshine split it with piercing rays of light. It was already past nine o'clock in the evening, but as the days rolled closer to midsummer, they stretched further and further until there was little night left at all.

Jussi Alonen strolled along the cobbled streets and turned the corner into the impressive Esplanadi Avenue. Despite the warmth of the evening, the summer crowds seemed thinner than usual, and it was a pleasant change for his way to be less crowded.

He set off down the street of Aleksanterinkatu towards the sea. On the way, he paused for a few moments, which allowed him to take in the view of the Tuomiokirkko. The impressive white Cathedral looked snow-white against the background of the summer sky. He smiled to himself, contented, as he continued onwards to the seafront.

It was Monday evening, and Jussi had arranged to meet an old friend from Rauma. They planned to meet up at a bar in the city centre. He already knew the place. It was on an old boat, moored against the harbour wall. It only had a few tables outside, but they were basking in the evening sun at that moment. Ice cold beer was also available, and Jussi was thirsty. As he continued to stroll towards the bar, he reflected on recent events.

It had been almost two months since his move to Helsinki. Following the circumstances surrounding a significant case in Rauma, he had been offered a promotion and relocation to Finland's capital city. 'The Paintings of Rauma' affair had involved theft and murder, amongst other crimes, and Jussi had been a leading figure in its resolution.

The case had centred on the theft of several paintings, with clues indicating the location of long-hidden valuables. After the treasure had been found, millions were exchanged, and gang members were shot and killed. Only Jussi's ex-girlfriend, Heli, had escaped. He hadn't known until later that she'd also been part of the gang. She had last been heard of, taking refuge in Cuba but had subsequently disappeared off the map.

Jussi still felt raw over his relationship with Heli. It was this, combined with his ambition to become a detective, that had finally prompted a change of scenery and a new life. It had been quite a change. From being a young police officer in uniform, he was now training to be a Detective. This had required a transfer to the police station in Pasila, part of Helsinki.

When the opportunity had been offered, he had struggled long and hard with his decision. He had been happy in Rauma. However, he discussed it with his superior, who had arranged a one-year secondment with a guaranteed position back in Rauma if he should wish to return. With his ambition to become a successful Detective ahead of him, there seemed only one direction in which to go.

◆ ◆ ◆

It was a pleasant evening, which started at the bar with a few beers and ended with some bowling at a nearby entertainment complex. They had even considered karaoke, but Jussi had to work the next day.

It had been good to meet up with one of his buddies from the police training school in Tampere and talk about old times, and newer ones. At the end of the evening, he said goodbye to his friend, who made his way towards the train station, as Jussi headed home.

As he walked, he crossed the tramlines of Mannerheimintie (Mannerheim Road) and strode into the attractive avenue of Bulevardi. He continued walking the remaining couple of blocks to the building that contained his apartment.

Jussi had decided to experience real Helsinki life and had been fortunate to find a small but ideally located studio apartment to rent in the city's centre. Opposite the apartment block, on his right, was a small park, currently smothered in green and adorned with colourful flowers. Jussi enjoyed the relaxation of the Vanha Kirkkopuisto (Old Church Park) and often walked through it on his way home.

On arrival, he looked upwards. Every time he returned, he never failed to be impressed by the building in which he had made his home, at least for a year. It was pale yellow and white, with the original Jugend design featured on its facade. Jussi tapped in his code on the keypad and entered the apartment block. He continued thinking as he walked up the stairs.

His first three months in Helsinki had certainly passed quickly. He had been swiftly launched into an investigation, which had left little space for a social life when combined with his training program.

However, he always tried to make the most of any gaps in his schedule. To this end, he had taken up kayaking. He had begun to visit the area around Vuosaari island on his days off. Sometimes, he would rent a kayak for a couple of hours and paddle around the small islands. He had also attended a kayaking course and participated in a couple of sightseeing tours with groups, which he had enjoyed.

Tomorrow, however, was a working day and soon after

entering his apartment, he went to bed.

◆ ◆ ◆

Jussi awoke early the following day, with sunlight streaming into the studio apartment. He reminded himself to buy some black-out curtains. He enjoyed his sleep too much to be awoken at 5 am by bright sunshine, searching out every available gap in his curtains.

The first job - make the coffee. Jussi and coffee were inseparable, and he enjoyed his potent brew. Sometimes, he would buy a cappuccino from one of the coffee shops downtown. Recently, he had also invested in his own impressive, retro-looking coffee machine from the department store. It ground the coffee beans itself and made a powerful espresso, as well as a perfect cappuccino on Sunday mornings.

After his quick breakfast, he got dressed, grabbed his bag and left the apartment for his commute to work.

Outside, Tuesday had delivered a perfect day. It was sunny with a light breeze of fresh air blowing in from the sea. He made his way to the central railway station, where he caught the train to Pasila. The journey took just over ten minutes.

In total, his commute was an easily manageable thirty minutes, from the door of his apartment to the steps of the police station. After that, it was time for coffee number two, with the usual greetings and conversations on the way to his desk on the third floor. That morning, he met his colleague Tapio in the small kitchen.

"Hyvää Huomenta Tapsa!" Jussi proffered. (Good Morning - Tapsa was his nickname).

Tapio returned the greeting with a broad smile. Then, poured out a second cup of black coffee, which was available 24/7 at the police station. It wasn't Jussi's favourite brew, but it was free-flowing and sustained him throughout the day.

Tapio was a little older than Jussi, in his late-30's, with fair hair, blue eyes and an almost permanent smile deeply engraved onto his face. He had been in the police force for his whole career and assigned to the detective unit for the past five years. As he already knew the ropes, he had been especially helpful to Jussi in his early days in Helsinki.

Jussi himself, full name Jussi Alonen, had dark hair and distinctive, dark-brown eyes, looking somewhat younger than his age of twenty-nine. He wore smart but modern clothes, usually in shades rather than colours and was often seen with his favourite black leather bag and laptop. He usually carried various gadgets due to his interest in new technology. In his free time, the bag often contained one of his cameras, which he enjoyed using to take photographs of nearby nature and city scenes.

Jussi's working day generally started with desk-top research. As he was training, he was typically assigned to the background work of investigations. Usefully, Jussi was adept at navigating the internet and using various digital platforms. He was already earning a reputation as someone who could be relied upon to provide the necessary information, insights or documents, needed in police investigations.

At the moment, he was working on a recent spike of bicycle thefts in the city. This was perhaps not the most exciting of cases, however, to many residents of Helsinki, bicycles were an essential mode of transport. The government was keen on promoting pedal-power to reduce traffic and emissions, and thefts of bicycles were not good news for this cause.

Furthermore, the victims had lost high-value items, including expensive electric bikes. Some of these would cost some thousands to buy, and was becoming a serious issue, so the case had been escalated to the Detective Investigation Unit.

Jussi spent the first part of the day piecing together the locations of the thefts. Then, the models, brands and values of the bicycles, together with their owner details, were added to a document.

This work continued after lunch, which had been a delicious salmon soup and ruisleipä (rye bread). After this, Jussi searched various marketplace websites. He wanted to check if any of the stolen bikes were available for sale. For many people, it wouldn't have been an exciting job, however, Jussi had taken to this kind of work as the crucial part of police investigation that it was. He considered it a sort of treasure hunt. He would often find a promising lead, deep within the unlimited pages of the internet.

During that afternoon, he spotted a possible pattern in the location of the thefts. He wandered over to Tapio's desk to discuss it, interrupting an apparent search of thin air.

"Tapsa, I may have a lead on these bike thefts."

Tapio looked at him with interest.

"Tell me more."

Jussi continued and explained his theory.

The bikes were usually taken in the mornings, from the outside of offices. These buildings had relatively hidden back yards or bike sheds, seemingly within a particular circuit. He had been able to view the locations from his desk, using a street-view site. Tapio agreed that the pattern deserved further investigation and approached the Detective Sergeant of their section, Pekka Virtanen.

Pekka listened carefully and studied the map.

"I think you've found something interesting, Jussi," he said, nodding his head.

Pekka suggested they take a trip downtown to check the places first-hand. Jussi and Tapio took the stairs down to the carpark and checked out one of the pool cars from the Facilities Manager. They pulled out onto the main road and headed towards the area of Jätkäsaari: the docklands area. Nearby were a growing number of offices that were served by bike -tracks from new apartment blocks.

They checked the area and took photographs. They also talked to some receptionists and security guards from some larger office buildings for further information. Jussi had previously visited one of the girls at one office to talk about security, and they exchanged some friendly banter.

After this task, they returned to the station, and Jussi typed their updates into the central computer system. From then on, they continued to check the for-sale pages on the internet against the daily updated list of recovered bikes. This information was subsequently shared with the uniformed division, who would increase patrols in these areas, thereby deterring further thefts.

Satisfied with his day's work and with the fact that no related issues had been reported, Jussi packed away his things and finished his day just before 6 pm. His days were quite regular these days when compared to his time in the uniformed division. However, he knew this would change after his training period when he would be on more active duty.

◆ ◆ ◆

Gregor Turgenev lived in an old restored mansion on the island of Krestovsky, part of a wealthy suburb of St Petersburg, Russia.

The pale blue building boasted gold and white marble decoration. It had well-kept gardens, in a French style, surrounded by a high wall. The mansion benefited from tight security, including a gatehouse, an inner control room with CCTV display and armed security guards at the gate. One of the ostentatious features of the mansion was a large glass orangery housing an indoor swimming pool with its own small private nightclub.

Gregor was unmarried now, with no children and several girlfriends. He enjoyed his lifestyle in his own way. He was in his 50's, tall, slim and generally seen in bright-coloured jackets and silk scarves. He liked to show off his wealth in an extravagant manner. He had a short grey beard, together with short grey hair and ice-blue eyes. He was social in public, but his mood could change. Not many would dare to make him angry and face those eyes and whatever consequences they may impose. Despite this, he was a generous man and enjoyed making other people wealthy, provided that things were done as agreed.

Gregor had been born into money with rich parents, and had spent much of his life growing more of it. He had found, through experience, that he could use his talents in a variety of ways to gain even more wealth in the new, post-Soviet Russia. Over the years, he had built up an impressive empire of real estate investments, many gained through criminal activities. He had built his organisation to enable him to grow various illegal activities, including theft, smuggling and people trafficking. He disliked online activities and preferred old fashioned hands-on crime, or at least for his associates to accomplish this for him.

After some trial and error, he had successfully franchised his criminal model. He self-christened the organization 'Gadyuki' which translated to 'Vipers.' In some states in Russia, he had provided partners with the finance and know-how to set up organizations that both relied upon and rewarded him. It was a profitable franchise arrangement with little risk on his part; however, it was not enough for him. He could see other opportunities elsewhere - the world was a big place.

Today, Gregor sat in his grand office, lovingly modelled on the Washington Whitehouse's oval office. He surveyed a map in front of him and looked up at his gathered associates. He addressed the small group in front of him, sitting along the table.

"Gentlemen - and lady," he added, his eye having been caught by the attractive female figure, dressed in yellow to his right. "Now that we have established a successful operation in Latvia, I believe we're now ready to expand into the Nordic countries. As we have already agreed, we will begin in Finland and take advantage of opportunities to grow the business in Sweden as and when they arise. Edgars, our Latvian Franchisee, will lead this expansion," he said, nodding at the slim figure dressed in a black suit to his right.

"I am thrilled to lead this new project," Edgars commented enthusiastically.

Gregor continued, "We will initially focus on the growing demand for boats, which will provide Edgars with the necessary funding for expansion. Then, he will use his resources to explore the potential for the entertainment industry. In our business plan, he will generate five million euros within the first year. We estimate this to require the theft of two boats per week, with an average selling price in Russia, of fifty-thousand euros. He will retain his 50% share of the profits and use my 50% share as an interest-free loan for the first two years. This arrangement will help him to get firmly established. After two years, any ventures established in Finland will result in the usual 25% franchise fee. You will all benefit from the usual percentage."

"What about the business in Latvia? Will it be left exposed?" asked the female figure in yellow.

Gregor cast his eye over to Natalja Ivanov, the lady sitting to his left. She was a striking woman, with her jet-black hair falling over a bright yellow, somewhat revealing dress. Natalja was Gregor's Head of Finance and the owner of the Russian Karelian franchise. She was keen to grow overall revenue and expand her own activities into Eastern Finland.

"The Finnish business will be run from Riga, at least initially, so I see no risk in our diversification. We can establish a satellite office in Helsinki during the first year and introduce other activities soon after. After this, we will move into Stockholm and expand across the Nordics at a rate of one country per year."

"When will we begin?" asked Natalja.

"We already have," answered Edgars, turning around to face her, smiling.

Natalja's lips curled only slightly to crease her usually stern expression. The other figures in the room nodded with approval. They included Gregor's Business Manager, Anatoly Koskinen, who was part-Finnish and equally keen to see this expansion proceed. Also present in the room were several other franchisees from other parts of Russia.

To enable harmony across his empire and avoid clashes, Gregor had brought in a system whereby his franchisees not only benefited heavily from their own revenue but also from a small share of everyone else's. This was not an attempt at socialism, merely to encourage a united effort to expand. The more development that took place, the more revenue he made from his royalties.

The meeting lasted most of the day. In the evening, discussions continued in Gregor's nightclub over champagne, oysters and caviar. Gregor stretched out in the jacuzzi at the end of the evening with a large cognac, satisfied after a productive day.

◆ ◆ ◆

In Helsinki, Jussi had plans for Tuesday evening. He was to return home and take his camera to the area of Vuosaari. He planned to rent a kayak and take photographs.

After arriving at his apartment, he decided to take his cheaper camera model, just in case of accidents. It was the first time he would take a camera with him, as by his own admission, he was not an expert paddler yet. Next, he changed clothes and collected his other gear. When he was ready, he took the train back to Helsinki centre.

Returning to the central train station, he took another train for a thirty minute journey, and walked the rest of the way. He didn't have his car in Helsinki as he had left it in Rauma, deciding that the southeast of Finland could easily be navigated by public transport. He didn't see the point in paying high carpark fees or struggling to find parking spaces either.

On arrival at the Waterports Centre, open late on summer nights, he arranged his kayak hire. He had thought of buying one several times but decided it was cheap enough and perhaps more convenient to rent one when needed.

"Hey Jussi! The usual one?" asked the man behind the desk, as Jussi walked over to the counter.

"Yes, that would be great, thanks," answered Jussi.

"I'll have to write your name on that one soon," the man joked.

On arrival at the beach, he looked at his chosen craft with satisfaction. It was a bright yellow sea kayak, definitely his favourite model so far.

After stowing his gear, he pushed off and glided smoothly across the water. His craft gained depth towards the centre of the straits, taking him towards the small islands.

Jussi appreciated the freedom he felt when paddling a kayak. Now, all he could hear was the whooshing sound of the craft moving forward as his paddles dipped into the water, alternately, at each side. The water was flat and calm tonight, so he was quickly propelled forward. It was a warm night, but the air that blew on his face was pleasantly cooler. He took in his surroundings as the seagulls rose into the air, squawking at his approach.

He paddled for a further fifteen minutes. Then, feeling relatively stable, he reached for his camera and removed it from the bag. This action wasn't as easy as it should have been, as he had methodically wrapped it in plastic to prevent water damage. However, after fumbling for a few minutes, he was finally ready and started to take pictures of the surrounding area.

As he slowly moved forward, carried by the current, he took photos of the nearby island. The spectacular sights included the mainland and the sea itself. The pictures were enhanced by the sun reflecting onto the water as it dropped lower in the sky.

There was some activity in the area as boats returned from an evening out. A few boats were setting off. They were mainly bow-runners, together with a few yachts under engine power. Tonight, the wind had dropped almost completely.

Jussi noted a sleek Sunseeker craft, obviously expensive, with people in swimsuits that looked ready to party. He smiled as they waved at him, and he waved back in return. Then he quickly covered his camera and replaced it into the kayak's cockpit. The expected wake from the boat tossed his kayak around on the waves for a while. After a couple of minutes, it was calm once again, so he continued to paddle towards the slowly sinking sun.

It was now getting close to ten o'clock, and he was keen to stretch out his time on the water until sunset. He paddled along the coast, staying close to the shore as the returning boat traffic increased. Some of the boats were quite large, and it was challenging to maintain stability through their wake.

Jussi stopped and took countless photographs of the surrounding area from time to time, using the continuous shooting mode. He liked to take as many pictures as possible and then enjoyed selecting the best ones at his leisure.

Boats glided effortlessly across the water as the sky started to blend into shades of orange. Jussi snapped away at the spectacular view.

Suddenly, he saw a splash to his left, about thirty metres away. He strained to see what had made it, and then he saw the perpetrator. A seal was chasing fish. It leapt out of the water, again and again, seemingly having fun. He couldn't believe his luck and clicked away until it disappeared.

The sun was now very low, and he stopped taking photographs for a moment to take in the view. It was stunning, and he couldn't have wished for a better end to his trip. It was getting late now, though, and he turned the kayak around and headed back to the watersports centre.

He arrived just after eleven o'clock and was surprised to see a party of people setting out at that time. Voices speaking English in various accents drifted clearly across the water.

It must be a sightseeing trip, he thought, as he arrived at the beach.

He returned the kayak and made his way towards home.

On the train, he flicked through the photographs on his camera and was pleased with the result of his evening's activity. He could still taste the salty sea air on his tongue, and his face felt fresh from the breeze. He would sleep well tonight.

◆ ◆ ◆

The next day, Jussi awoke a little later. His shift was due to start and end later on that day. The plan was to continue the bike-theft investigation, with some time spent around the circuit he had previously identified as a hot spot.

Sometimes, Jussi would visit the café across the road in Bulevardi Avenue for breakfast and have something from the bakery counter, together with a frothy cappuccino. This had often been his routine in Rauma, when his schedule had allowed it, and he had been keen to find a replacement café in Helsinki. He had settled on an old traditional place that, although Finnish, reminded him of a café in Vienna. He had visited Austria some years back with an ex-girlfriend. He liked modern coffee shops, however, this particular café had an air of sophistication about it that somehow made him feel more immersed in the whole Helsinki experience.

On arrival, he was greeted by a girl behind the counter.

"Huomenta Jussi, Mitä kuuluu?" (Good Morning Jussi, how are you?).

Jussi smiled and returned the greeting. He had become familiar with Kirsty over the past couple of months. Seeing her smile was another excellent reason to visit the café. After exchanging a few words with each other, he took a seat. As was his habit, he spent time checking the news on his phone while he ate breakfast.

When he had finished, he left to do some shopping at the small supermarket nearby. He then completed a few other minor tasks before beginning his working day.

◆ ◆ ◆

At the Police Station, Jussi was once again busy with his research. He was checking through the latest list of reported crimes in Uusimaa (the region of South Finland). There was little crime at present. However, there was a small selection of stolen cars and drink or drug-related problems. There was nothing new on bike thefts, but instead, a boat had disappeared.

That's unusual, Jussi thought, studying the report closely.

It seemed that a speedboat had been reported stolen from the harbour during the previous evening. The boat was expensive, with a replacement insurance value of almost 100,000 euros.

A voice arose from over his shoulder.

"I wonder how they managed to steal that one and calmly steer out to sea?" asked Tapio.

"I was wondering the same thing," replied Jussi. "It's strange. Boat thefts are rare, although I know there have been a few this year. They are so difficult to conceal and sell forward in Finland. Especially something as expensive as that."

They chatted for a while, after which they made their way to the pool car garage and drove downtown. Perhaps today, they would find and arrest their bicycle thief?

THE HARBOUR

It was afternoon, and Jussi strolled along the harbour front, marvelling at some of the boats moored there.

Some of these must be worth more than I make in a decade, he thought.

Jussi eyed up an imposing model with twin decks, and wondered what it must be like inside.

The stolen bike investigation was continuing, but they had been asked to support this new case, as it involved a valuable boat. The two detectives did this by interviewing boat owners and harbour staff.

As his mentor strode alongside him, Jussi noted that Tapio was seemingly uninterested in the larger boats but took a deeper interest in smaller motor launches. He observed him consider a particular one and recalled that Tapio had mentioned he was considering buying a boat.

"Hey, Tapsa!" Jussi called over.

Tapio returned to reality and replied.

"What?"

"Do you still have boat fever?" Jussi teased.

Tapio laughed and walked over to him as they continued walking along the path by the sea.

They had arranged to meet the owners of the stolen vessel at a nearby café. They had decided it would be easier to interview everyone concerned at the scene of the crime. Perhaps this would provide some new insights.

The detectives arrived at the café and identified the owners. The couple were relatively young, obviously wealthy and very anxious about the theft. After everyone had introduced themselves, the questions began.

Tapio began, "Thank you for meeting with us. I understand that you have already been through some questions. We have been asked to support this investigation due to the high value of this particular theft."

They covered the boat's security details, the frequency of use, who may have had access, and other vital questions. The vessel had GPS, but clearly, this had been disabled. It had been used a few days before the theft and then moored as usual, in the same place as it had been for the past three years, without issue.

At the end of the interview, they thanked the couple for their cooperation and left. The conversation with the Harbour Master on duty yielded little more in terms of helpful information. It turned out that the thieves knew what they were doing and had disabled the CCTV system prior to the theft taking place.

With nothing new to follow-up, the two detectives concluded the evening by doing a patrol around the bicycle theft circuit. Next, they returned to the station to write the report. At least there had been no more bike thefts in the last couple of days.

"Perhaps, the perpetrators have realised the area is under surveillance?" asked Jussi.

"Or maybe they've been put off by knowing we are now on the case?" Tapio replied with a grin.

They were starting to pack up to leave when Tapio received a call on his radio. What Jussi heard next was most unexpected.

"Jussi. You're not going to believe this, but another boat has been stolen." Tapio announced.

"What?"

"That's odd. Two in as many days. When did it happen?"

"The owners are not sure. They've just returned from a holiday in Greece. They decided to take the boat out this afternoon, and it isn't there anymore," Tapio answered, then continued, "Okay, we have the case. Come on, unless you have other plans, that is?" he asked Jussi with a smile.

Jussi returned the smile and inwardly became quite excited about the prospect of a more interesting case. They made their way back to the harbour to meet uniformed officers at the scene, who would brief them.

Tapio relayed that a message had arrived from above that the thefts of expensive boats needed to stop. In addition, those stolen had to be recovered without delay. It seemed that messages from some prominent people had been sent, concerned about the security of their own boats.

The detectives approached the situation in the same way as before and had conversations with the owner and harbour master, who had been unaware of the theft until informed.

It seemed that this particular boat had two moorings: one in Helsinki and one near the couples' home further along the coast. It was not unusual for it to be missing from its Helsinki mooring.

In addition to compiling their report, they ascertained, as much as practical, if other boats could be missing. It appeared that the answer was no but without absolute certainty due to the fluidity of boating life.

Jussi and Tapio completed the interviews and added the

results to their notebooks. They returned to the station and added the information to the shared database. There hadn't been much in the way of additional facts gathered by the uniformed division. Still, police work was often a battle of information. The more information everyone had on a case, the better chance of discovering a clue to resolve it.

◆ ◆ ◆

It had been a more extended day than expected, and after bidding his farewells to those remaining, Jussi made his way home.

During the journey to central Helsinki, he realized he had nothing in his fridge, which wasn't uncommon for him. He didn't feel like shopping or cooking, so decided to stop at a sushi place he had visited a few times. He walked to the Kamppi area of Helsinki and through the large shopping centre.

It was later now, so everything was quieter. Jussi walked through the other side of the centre and crossed the small square to the restaurant. He was surprised to find it was bustling inside.

"Moi!" (Hi) said the smiling waitress as he stepped inside.

"Moi!" he replied. "Do you have a table for one?"

"It's jam-packed right now, but I'll find a table for you if you'd like to take a seat? It could be about half an hour, though. Or, if it would be okay, I could seat you at the big table? I just need to check with the lady sitting there," she offered helpfully.

Jussi glanced over to the table and saw an attractive girl, probably a few years younger than him. She had honey blonde hair tied back with a pretty braid on one side. She was looking at her smartphone with a wry smile, seemingly studying something interesting. Some progress had already been made with a large plate of sushi that sat in front of her. Jussi agreed to take a seat at the large table, provided it was okay with the incumbent diner.

The waitress walked over and said something to the girl. She looked up and smiled at him, with her head to one side. Then, she nodded.

"Sure, fine," she mouthed - or something like that, Jussi guessed.

Jussi removed his lightweight jacket, placed it on the hanger and made himself comfortable. He took a menu that had been placed in front of him and began to study it.

"The salmon sashimi is delicious," a voice said.

Jussi looked up. What he saw made him smile. The girl was considering him with her coy smile and a pair of incredible green eyes. He was stumped for a moment and didn't know what to say. He wanted to say how amazing her eyes were but suddenly realised how cliché it might sound.

Instead, he replied, "Really? In that case, I may have to order some."

She smiled - even longer this time.

"Why don't you try one of mine? I've ordered far too much. I wasn't that hungry when I arrived but got carried away by the picture on the menu. It all looked so good."

"Thanks. I don't mind if I do," replied Jussi.

Jussi took his chopsticks and snapped them apart. It didn't go exactly to plan, as he managed to snap one of the sticks in half, sending one half of them flying across the dining room.

The girl laughed and passed him another set from across the table, which he accepted somewhat sheepishly. He took one of the sashimi pieces from her plate. It was comprised of thin fresh salmon sitting on top of sticky white rice, bound with a green strip of something. He tasted it and found it to be delicious. He looked up and found that the girl was still studying him.

"This sounds corny, but I think we've met somewhere before," she said. "Have we?"

He returned her gaze, which he didn't find difficult and suddenly realized.

"Yes, of course. You tested my eyes a couple of months ago for my new job!"

At this, they both smiled even more broadly as they remembered.

When Jussi had first arrived in Helsinki from Rauma, one of the things that he had been asked to do was to have a new eye examination. An appointment had been made at an Optical store in the city. An attractive young Optometrist had examined his eyes, and everything was in order. They had spoken about his new job, and Jussi would have been very interested in spending more time talking to her. However, the situation at the optical store had felt a little awkward.

Now, the same girl was sitting right in front of him, and she introduced herself for the second time.

"Hi, I'm Selma."

"Hi, I'm Jussi," he said, as they shook hands in an official mock kind of way.

The pair continued to talk. In the end, Jussi just shared her food and ordered a chilled bottle of Riesling to accompany it. It was the most enjoyable evening he had spent since arriving in the city. They talked and talked and talked. It was one of those times when two people meet, and the conversation flows so naturally that neither one has to think about what to say next. Then, all of a sudden, it was closing time. They drained their wine glasses, left the restaurant and stood in front of each other.

"Okay, it seems that you need to go that way - and I have to go this way," said Selma, with a mock sad expression.

"Yes, I live just over there in Bulevardi, and you?" Jussi asked.

"Oh, I live over there, in Kallio."

She gestured somewhere into the distance.

"It doesn't take long for me to come into the centre, though, if you want to meet up again sometime?"

This would've been Jussi's question, but he was happier that she had asked it. Next, they exchanged mobile phone numbers and kissed each other lightly on the cheek. They waved to each other twice as Selma turned around and walked a few steps backwards before turning the corner and disappearing.

◆ ◆ ◆

The following day, Jussi awoke and smiled at the memory of an enjoyable evening. Another reason to be happy was that today was a day off.

He started his coffee machine and showered quickly. Then, he looked out of the window and groaned. Overnight, the expected blue sky of summer had changed into a grey overcast one, adding a drizzle of rain as an added insult.

Jussi had planned to take a kayak out again, but now he didn't feel so enthusiastic about the idea. As he drained his coffee, he decided it would be a good idea to spend a relaxing morning at his apartment instead. He took so many pictures these days; he had a problem arranging them so they didn't disappear into a digital bin, never to be seen again. Today, he would set up a new folder on his desktop entitled Kayak Trips and get it done. He would review the photographs he had taken and select the best ones to add to his digital collection.

He shaved and put on his favourite loungewear, comprising a white t-shirt, soft grey hoodie and college-style trousers. After this, he poured more coffee into an oversized mug, took a notebook and sat down on his small sofa, with the oval table in front of him. He began the transfer of his photographs from both of his cameras to his laptop. He hadn't done this for some time, so he guessed it was going to take a while.

Jussi had furnished his chosen apartment quite simply, partly because it was a rental arrangement and partly as he had kept his place in Rauma. The room was predominantly white, with grey kitchen units and all appliances built-in. There was also a modern white bathroom. He had added white curtains, a blue sofa, a small white oval table, a double bed, a small round white dining table with two chairs decorated with blue cushions, and a blue rug. Some of his favourite photographs decorated the walls: some in colour, some black and white. Overall, the room was modern but had a nautical hint, which suited Helsinki. He hadn't intended it like that but approved of the result.

Jussi sat on the sofa while the final pictures finished transferring. Then, he remembered something and did the same thing with his mobile phone.

Soon he was relaxing back on the cushions and flipping through the photographs. One by one, he went through the pictures, keeping the good ones and deleting the bad ones. He smiled every so often or frowned and occasionally considered one critically as he reviewed them.

There were almost two thousand photographs to deal with, and he was a little annoyed with himself for not doing this sooner. He was usually very efficient in this regard; however, the new job and things on his mind had prevented him from taking the time for the task.

He stopped for a moment and studied one of the pictures. The picture was of Heli, his ex-girlfriend, well, kind of girlfriend. A few months ago, he had been involved with her again but felt she had used him for her own purposes. She had been part of a gang involved in crimes associated with 'The Paintings of Rauma' case. Despite the situation, he still harboured fond memories of her and remembered the call he had received from her while in Stockholm. She had apologised for everything. He considered the photograph for a moment and almost pressed 'delete' but didn't quite follow through. He moved it into a folder marked Heli and moved on with his task.

Jussi was satisfied with the quality of many of the photos and sometimes nodded or smiled as he regarded them. He enjoyed viewing the images taken from his Kayak in particular. There were some spectacular ones of sunsets and nature in the area. He looked at one specific picture where the trees were perfectly mirrored in the water's reflection. He decided that this one would find its way onto the wall in his apartment and highlighted it accordingly.

He continued like this for some time, placing them methodically into appropriate sub-folders in his computer. He finally finished his task a little before lunchtime.

"Right. Time for lunch!" he announced to himself.

It had been a job well done, and he decided to return to the same Sushi place for lunch. He tidied everything away. This was necessary because the studio apartment was relatively small, and it didn't take much to cause a mess. Jussi was a tidy person, although not overly so. He just liked his place to look bright, modern, minimalist and uncluttered.

He Looked outside: the day was bright and sunny now, although not quite so warm. It was going to be a fine afternoon. He dressed lightly and casually in a blue polo shirt, jeans, a tan lightweight sweater and brown loafers. Lastly, he added his latest accessory, his smartwatch, which kept track of his daily steps, with his new goal being ten thousand per day.

It's time to make a hole in that target, he decided.

He jogged down the stairs and opened the door into the daylight. He walked across the street and headed in the direction of Kamppi, walking through the park as he did so. He turned around briefly and looked at the building where he lived, admiring it as usual.

A few minutes later, he arrived at the restaurant. Again, it was busy. However, the same waitress who had welcomed him before smiled and found him a small table at one side of the room.

Jussi ordered a small plate of sushi plus a beer, as it was his day off. The room was full of the usual lunchtime clientele, busy professionals, students and the occasional tourist. The gender was predominantly female. He had thought this on previous occasions and wondered why for a moment, although he secretly approved. He half-expected Selma to walk in, but unfortunately, she didn't. What the experience did prompt him to do, was to call her on his way back from the restaurant.

Selma's mobile phone was set to answerphone, which he expected as she had explained that she was fully booked with patients all day at the optical store. He left a voice message.

"Hi, It's Jussi. I've just been for sushi again, and it reminded me of our chance meeting at the restaurant last night. Perhaps we could meet on purpose next time? How about tomorrow evening?"

Then he went to the department store on the corner and browsed for a new shirt for the occasion as he was confident that Selma would accept his offer. He selected a stylish but casual white cotton shirt with a well-placed logo. Next, he visited the delicatessen and made some purchases to restock his fridge.

Afterwards, Jussi returned home and spent the remaining part of the day doing some chores. He needed to catch up on his emails, pay a few bills and iron a few shirts. He ended the day by watching an episode of a British detective serial he was following.

He was just about to turn into bed when a text message alert beeped on his phone. It was Selma.

Hey Jussi, thanks for your message and the invitation. Happy to meet up tomorrow evening. You choose the place. 7 o'clock? Selma.

Jussi smiled and texted back.

7 pm. It's a date.

FOUND ADRIFT

Jussi awoke to sunlight streaming into his apartment once again. It was 5.32am. He reminded himself, again, to buy some proper curtains or blinds. Nonetheless, he appreciated the sun that morning as it provided an energy boost to prepare for the day ahead.

When he was ready, he strolled out of the building with a spring in his step. Propelled by a combination of sunlight, strong coffee and a future date with Selma, he felt unbeatable.

At the station, it seemed many of his colleagues were away from the office. Looking out of the window, Jussi couldn't blame them. Tapio had been called out to help with something already and so he attended the weekly station briefing, together with some of his colleagues. There was the usual assortment of 'run of the mill' incidents. However, one particular and rather grim event was of great interest to all.

A uniformed sergeant, named Tommi, announced, "A stolen boat was recovered last night, containing a deceased male."

This statement caused considerable murmurs around the conference room.

He continued, raising his voice.

"The boat was stolen on Tuesday evening and only found last night, adrift at sea. The male occupant has not yet been identified, however, we believe him to be Latvian in origin, according to a document he had in his possession. The post mortem is pending but the initial inspection suggests that he died of a single gunshot wound to the chest."

After questions about the victim, someone asked, "How many boats have been stolen this year now?'"

Tommi replied, "In total, there have been seven thefts in and around Helsinki. The latest one was a particularly high value model. None of the other vessels have been recovered."

Someone else asked, "Don't all boats have GPS?"

"Yes, but it seems it was disabled on this boat, rendering it less visible."

More questions followed but there was little additional information available at that point. The matter was concluded with the statement that a task force would soon be established, with the members announced shortly. The briefing ended soon afterwards.

Jussi left the briefing and almost walked into Tapio as he turned the corner.

"Hey, what's the rush Jussi?" he asked good-naturedly.

Jussi verbally downloaded the contents of the briefing and asked Tapio what he thought the chances were of them being assigned to the case. Tapio conjectured that as they were already involved in the boat theft case, it seemed logical they would be added to the team.

In fact, it wasn't long before they heard some news on that very subject. They were standing in the small kitchen, discussing the models of boats that had been stolen, over a coffee, when their senior officer, Inspector Jonas Nieminen, joined them.

"Good Morning! Were you talking about boats?"

"Yes, said Jussi, it seems most of the stolen boats were of a similar type: expensive, medium-sized, with powerful engines. Fast enough to get away but non-descript enough to sell onwards."

"Interesting," the Inspector nodded, "And why do you think our male victim was shot?"

"Possibly a deal gone bad?" Tapio suggested.

The Inspector nodded, not quite agreeing but not quite disagreeing either.

"Anyway," he continued. "I would like both of you on the task force. There have been too many boats stolen this year and the case has now been passed to us. Pekka will head this one up and I think, Jussi, this is going to be great experience for you."

Jussi and Tapio nodded in agreement and the Inspector left them to digest the news. They decided that lunch time was the perfect time to discuss it. Especially as today the lunch restaurant had a rare treat on the menu, a favourite Finnish speciality of venison, berries and mash.

◆ ◆ ◆

The harbour had been busy that day. Even though it was still a working week and not yet the holidays. Many people had seized the opportunity of enjoying the fine day by taking their boats out to the islands. A light breeze in the afternoon had also prompted a few sailing boats to join the selection of motor boats headed out to sea.

One of the boats contained a crew that had a very different plan in mind. The Helmsman of the *Wave Rider* was Hemmo Saarinen. He was joined by Samuli Isoranta. They were both from Helsinki. Hemmo was as skilled with boats as he was with cars, which was quite expert indeed. Samuli was basically hired muscle and no stranger to violent crime. He was often armed.

There had been a third member of the crew but he was now deceased, having been recovered by the police, the night before.

Today, they were surveying the variety of marine craft passing by, as they sat drinking a cold beer from the cooler on the deck. Their boat was a powerful so-called 'Go-fast Boat,' which was capable of outrunning almost anything on waves. It's four engines were monstrosities of power and Hemmo enjoyed opening them up to at least half-speed whenever he could. This was already faster than most boats in the area could hope to reach with everything they had.

The conversation on-deck was currently centered around a medium-sized bow-runner that looked quite new and had been fitted with two powerful outboard motors.

"That one would be a perfect choice," remarked Edgars, as he observed the craft through his binoculars.

"Yes, it would," agreed Hemmo as he followed it with his own set of binoculars.

Then, after a pause, Samuli leaned back, "So, what do you think of Edgars?" he asked.

Hemmo turned around and replied.

"He seems okay and the money arrives as it should do. It's his Boss that is best to stay clear of."

"Who's that?" Samuli asked.

"I think his name is Gregor. He's old-school Russian Mafia from St Petersburg. He's the leader of the organisation that Edgars works for. They call themselves 'The Vipers.' Nice eh? Anyway, we should keep our noses down and stick to taking boats and making money. Let's leave them to their own devices. Hopefully, they won't destroy too much of the world in the process."

Samuli agreed, sat back on the soft seating at the stern and took another slug of his beer. It was not his strong point to discuss tactics but to simply execute whatever needed doing. He was good at that.

◆ ◆ ◆

On Tuesday evening, Hemmo and Samuli's activities had been of a different nature. Andres Janesone had been the third member of their crew. He was a Latvian whom they had recruited to take some of the more riskier steps towards acquiring boats. He had been paid a thousand euros for every one and things had gone well with the first few boats. They had made a good three-man team, for a while.

On that fateful Tuesday evening, while scouting for a new target, Andres had boarded a suitable craft and Hemmo and Samuli joined him to steal it.

Further along the coast, they had spotted a coastguard patrol and decided to hide the boat. They drove it to a small pier and left it there, afterwards going their separate ways. However, unbeknown to Hemmo and Samuli, Andres had discovered a haul of drugs stashed below deck. He couldn't believe his eyes and estimated the value to be tens of thousands of euros. Now he had an great opportunity and decided to take the boat and the drugs and disappear. He started to move but was unaware that Hemmo always hid a special tracker in each stolen boat. When Hemmo had checked the app on his phone, he noted it was on the move.

Hemmo and Samuli immediately met at the harbour in Helsinki. They took their fast boat and raced out to sea, tracking the signal. Within a short time, they caught up with Andres. After a short chase and an even shorter argument, Samuli had shot him dead in the boat where he stood. The two thieves were amazed to find the haul inside and removed it, while leaving the body in the boat and the scene at speed. It had been found adrift by a yacht returning to the harbour. The coastguard and police arrived on the scene soon afterwards.

◆ ◆ ◆

Helsinki seemed to be moving towards its summer slumber, as the number of people in the city had already started to decline, leaving for their various holiday destinations. This was tempered by an increase in international tourists, however, the decrease was still obvious. Commensurate with the reduction of people, so also did crime reduce. It seemed the criminal fraternity took their vacations at the same time as law-abiding citizens.

That day, neither boat nor bicycle was stolen. The station had become quieter as the rotation of holidays began. It would be midsummer soon, and Jussi himself was keen to leave the city for a while and get out into the countryside. He was looking forward to partaking in some of the typical Finnish summertime lakeside pursuits of sauna, swimming, sausages and beer.

◆ ◆ ◆

It was Friday, and tonight would be Jussi's date with Selma. He was keen to see her again. Between one thing and another, they had both been busy and hadn't contacted each other since their initial texts. He decided to send her a message in the morning with the prospective venue for the evening.

Hey Selma, Let's meet at the Torni Bar at 7 pm and go for dinner at the Italian place on Esplanadi?

Within a couple of minutes, Selma replied.

Mojitos! Great! See you then.

Jussi was delighted to see that she shared his liking for Mojitos. He smiled as he put away his mobile phone. Tapio caught his expression as he put his phone away.

"Ah-ha, so Jussi has a date tonight," Tapio ribbed him.

Jussi muttered something appropriately derogatory to him, and they both laughed on their way to their desks.

◆ ◆ ◆

It was a busy day at City View Opticians and Selma was fully-booked with eye-test appointments. The text from Jussi made her day go even better and she started to sing to herself, quietly between patients. She didn't sing quietly enough though and her receptionist winked at her, knowingly, as she walked past the desk to the eye examination room. Selma opened her eyes wide with a mock-scolding expression and chuckled to herself.

Almost the weekend.

◆ ◆ ◆

Over at the harbour, the warm, welcoming air of Friday evening had prompted a plethora of boats to take to the water. The sun was shining in the sky and was likely to be doing so until late. Picnics and beer were stowed and groups of young people and families, lowered themselves into their boats. Everywhere, engines could be heard starting-up. Restaurants, bars and sauna terraces started to fill, all around the city. Boat traffic was busy going to and fro' but was mostly outward bound, as everyone wanted to make the most of such a fine evening.

In his apartment, Jussi spent more time than usual getting himself ready and when he was satisfied, left for his date.

DATE NIGHT

Jussi arrived at the Bar on the top floor of the hotel. He was wearing his new shirt, combined with smart jeans. He hadn't brought a jacket as it was even warmer than expected for the season, and the evening was set to remain at twenty degrees or more. He was a little early, so he ordered a beer and took a seat near the window to catch up on his emails and social media.

During that day, there had been a conference call. The detectives were updated on the report from the forensics team about the recovered body. The victim had been shot on board the boat due to the amount of blood spatter found. The estimated time of death was between Tuesday and Wednesday evening that week. Aside from the recovered paper in Latvian, which turned out to be a flyer for a pizza takeaway, there were no more details available about the victim. For the moment, it was just a strange body in a stolen boat.

Jussi sat looking through the window of the bar at the panoramic view, thinking through the day's events in his head. He wasn't paying attention to anything around him.

"Hey!"

A familiar voice announced from above, bringing him swiftly back to reality. He looked up and smiled. It was Selma. If she had looked attractive in the restaurant that night, now she looked stunning. He couldn't help himself taking in the view for a few moments. His attention was evident to Selma, and she smiled the biggest smile she could, with her green eyes sparkling. Jussi pulled himself together and stood up apologetically.

"Hey Selma, how are you? It's nice to see you! How was your day? Would you like a drink?"

"That's a lot of questions to answer. Should I start with a mojito? And let's take the rest as it comes."

Jussi nodded and replied, "Of course!"

He made his way to the bar. He couldn't understand why he had fluffed his lines again. He was usually so confident. He resolved to take a breath, calm down and takes things a little slower.

They enjoyed their drinks while catching up on the last few days. Both had been busy working most of the time, except for Jussi's day off.

As their conversation progressed, they discussed each other's hobbies. Selma was intrigued about his photography and spent a few minutes scanning through some of the shots on Jussi's phone.

"You're a very talented photographer, Jussi. I'm impressed. You didn't mention that you had hidden talents in our last conversation."

"Well, it's just an occasional hobby, but it's growing. I'm beginning to think about having an exhibition one day."

"You should. Really, you should. Not everyone has this kind of an eye for a picture," Selma remarked.

"I imagine not everyone has the eye to be an Optometrist either," Jussi responded, provoking a laugh from Selma.

They talked for a while about their respective chosen professions and then noticed the time.

"Hey, it's time to go," Jussi said.

They set off to the restaurant, down the narrow metal spiral staircase and took the old lift, together with a group of Japanese holiday-makers, down to the bottom floor. They looked and smiled at each other across the silence as the lift slowly creaked its way down to the lobby.

They walked to the restaurant, down the main street and across Esplanadi Avenue. They crossed the park where several picnickers were relaxing on benches and lying on the grass with blankets, enjoying the warmth of the evening.

They arrived at the restaurant, and the Maître d' showed them to their table. Once settled, their conversation resumed.

"So, how long have you been single?" asked Selma directly.

They briefly discussed their previous relationships, with neither giving too much away. Jussi decided to save the story about Heli and 'The Paintings of Rauma' for another day.

The evening went well once again, and this time it was enhanced by delicious Italian food. They both ate crunchy bruschetta, to begin with, followed by fresh Ravioli with spicy tomato sauce. They finished dinner with chocolate gelato and tiny but powerful espressos. Sighing with satisfaction at the meal and the company, Jussi was already wondering about a second date.

"Have you tried kayaking before, Selma?" he asked.

"Well, yes, a couple of times on vacation," she replied.

"Did you enjoy the experience? Might you be interested in coming along with me sometime? I mean, would you like to go together?" Jussi asked, slightly awkwardly.

"Yes, I would love to. When can we go?"

Jussi was delighted with her response and suggested they meet on the coming Sunday. He would pick her up from her apartment, hire kayaks at the usual place, and take her on an island tour. Selma loved the idea and suggested they lengthen the trip and take a picnic with them. They planned their day, for a little longer, as the waiter topped up their glasses with the remainder of the red wine from the bottle, chatting a little more about random things. It wasn't until the restaurant began to close that they left.

Selma linked her arm to his as they walked back along Esplanadi. The fine historic street looked resplendent as the sunset painted the old buildings with a burnt orange glow.

"Let's go to the sea," proposed Selma.

They turned around and walked towards the sea, finding a bench overlooking the harbour. The couple sat and talked while watching the view of the sunset splashing around the port and silhouetting some of the old buildings. After a few moments, they kissed.

◆ ◆ ◆

Meanwhile, a little further along the coast, a different kind of encounter was taking place. Two men were sitting at a café near the harbour, watching the sunset and waiting for the area to empty of people. This happened a little before midnight as the café began to close and the summer evening drew to a close.

"Let's go?" proposed Hemmo.

"Sounds good," answered Samuli and drained his coffee.

They walked over to the harbour wall, and Hemmo leaned casually against it. Samuli took some equipment from his bag, and they walked over to their target for the evening. Samuli boarded the vessel whilst Hemmo lit a cigarette and kept watch.

After a little technical work on the ignition and navigation panel, Samuli signalled Hemmo that all was ready. Hemmo stepped aboard and started the engine, and they carefully reversed the boat out of its dock, pointing its stern out of the harbour. Within ten minutes of entering the craft, Samuli slowly opened up its powerful twin engines and headed out to sea.

◆ ◆ ◆

Jussi and Selma finally rose from the bench and watched as a lone boat disappeared into the night. They made their way back along Esplanadi Avenue and arrived at the subway station. Selma gave Jussi a long lingering goodnight kiss and left to make her way home on the final train of the night. It had been a successful evening - and not just for Helsinki's latest couple.

THE ISLAND

Saturday arrived and Jussi had a few chores to do. One of those was a monthly visit to the supermarket, where he would buy what he needed to fill his fridge and cupboards. He usually made this major shopping trip on a weekend, so he would only need to grab a few essentials during the week. On this occasion, he also wanted to buy a few items from the local department store's delicatessen for the picnic on Sunday.

After completing this task, he visited a sports store, where he purchased a couple of dry bags for provisions. He would be able to use these on Sunday, and they would also come in useful for future trips. He also invested in some special waterproof pouches, one for his mobile phone and another for his camera. Next on his list was a visit to a book store, where he bought a detailed nautical map of the area, showing the islands and routes surrounding them.

Feeling the urge for coffee, he decided to visit the café inside the book store. After he had made himself comfortable, he opened the map and studied it over an iced cappuccino. Tracing with his finger, he located his usual route and followed it onwards to find a small passage through one of the smaller islands to the other side. He thought this might be worth exploring with Selma. For sure, they would find a picnic spot on the way or else somewhere on the island.

❖ ❖ ❖

That evening, after shopping, Jussi just felt like having an evening on the sofa. He switched on some music and decided to prepare for the next day with Selma. Firstly, he reviewed the map once more and marked the route. Next, he arranged his various dry bags and pouches on the floor. Then, he added his camera equipment and other items he considered essential for the expedition. Sticky notes were added to each dry bag to remind him of what food and drinks he should remember to pack. It was not an early morning ahead, but he didn't want to forget anything. He had planned a perfect day.

After this preparation, Jussi placed some popcorn into the microwave, took a cold beer from the fridge and selected an action film that had just been released. He didn't often watch television, but he enjoyed movies. He had recently installed a projector and sound system, so the screen rolled down with a press of the button, and he settled in for the evening.

◆ ◆ ◆

At the police station, things were not quite as relaxed. The central communication desk had received an emergency call that someone was in the process of stealing another boat. They dispatched a car and alerted the coast guard, who, in turn, contacted one of their patrol boats to intercept. A helicopter had also been placed on standby. Uniformed officers arrived at the harbour, and a small group of people had gathered by the sea wall - one of them waved at the officers who strode over to them.

"Someone has taken our boat!" a man shouted angrily.

One of the officers calmed him down and started to gather ownership information, together with a description of the vessel's type, size and colour. Having obtained the details, she radioed the coast guard and briefed them.

The officers were joined by another police car to begin

the process of interviewing witnesses, taking statements and pulling together the information required for the report and, hopefully, later, a prosecution. One of the other officers started to locate possible CCTV footage, which they could review later. Aside from this, there was little chance of recovering the boat from the harbour, as it had already left. This task was now in the hands of the Coast Guard.

Two hours later, despite a search involving a helicopter sweep over the coast, nothing had been found.

◆ ◆ ◆

Jussi awoke the following day at 8 am to the sound of his alarm. As was his habit, he checked his mobile phone for any messages that may require attention.

He was surprised to learn of the update describing the latest boat theft. Reading the circumstances, it seemed that the thieves had taken a significant risk this time. If the robbery had been spotted earlier, they could have been apprehended.

Jussi had already done some research on the value of these boats. A quick mental calculation concluded that the value of the thefts so far this year had already exceeded half a million euros.

"This is getting out of hand!" he exclaimed to the wall, after reading the message.

The announcement also informed that the local uniformed division had taken statements and concluded an unsuccessful search for the craft. Now, there would be more pressure from various directions to increase security and recover the missing boats. This would be exerted from boat owners, their associations, insurance companies, the council and even the Mayor of Helsinki.

The message stated that the crime prevention team had

already been in touch with the Harbour Master to discuss security precautions. Many of the boat owners had been contacted to provide practical tips on securing their vessels. Unfortunately, many were either unavailable or had been visiting the area from elsewhere. In addition, police patrols had been increased. These patrols were now completing a circuit at least every hour, and an unmarked car was being stationed at random locations.

Jussi noted another message advising him that a task force meeting had been arranged on Monday morning. It was now apparent that the following week would be a busy one. Solutions would need to be found for the continuing criminal activity. With this on his mind, he tried to focus back on his Sunday.

I should make the most of this weekend, he thought to himself.

He made a strong espresso and ate some muesli while packing his bags with food, drinks and other supplies.

When he had finished breakfast, he showered, shaved, brushed his teeth and dressed in lightweight clothes. Today would be a hot one, but the wind could be fresh on the water, so he took a light sweater and windcheater jacket just in case.

Okay. Now I'm ready.

He collected the bags and made his way out of the building. Walking down Bulevardi, he immediately felt the sun on his face. It was going to be a great day. He had that Sunday feeling when there was no rush to do anything except enjoy himself. He walked onwards to the railway station and estimated he would arrive on the coast at 9.30 am. There would be plenty of time to arrange the kayak rental and await Selma.

◆ ◆ ◆

Hemmo and Samuli were sitting outside a small coffee shop,

in the Kallio district of Helsinki. They were having a relaxing Sunday as well, with a successful week behind them, although one incident still disturbed them.

"I still don't understand why he would risk stealing that boat? I know the drugs were there but surely, he knew what kind of risk he would be taking. If we hadn't silenced him, then others probably would have," said Samuli.

Hemmo sighed.

"For some people, the money for a job is never enough. He just got greedy or felt that the stuff on the boat was worth trying to double-cross us for."

"I think there may already be too many people involved in this. Who knows who is involved from Latvia or Russia? We can't trust anyone now," commented Samuli.

"It's hard to trust criminals, Samuli," replied Hemmo. "By our nature, we're all dishonest, you know," he commented, laughing. Then added, "I'm sure you'll enjoy spending the bonus we found that night anyway."

Samuli smiled.

"Well, he won't be doing it again, that's for sure. I just wish we could have recovered the boat as well."

"Me too. It was a nice one, but we had to get away from there as quickly as possible. Let's make sure that in future, we don't leave anyone else alone with our boat. At least, not until we have searched it ourselves."

Samuli grunted in agreement.

◆ ◆ ◆

Jussi's calculations were correct, and he was already waiting on the beach with two kayaks when Selma arrived. He had been a little concerned that she would come with nice clothes and perfect hair, as this was how he had seen her each time. Kayaking called for more casual and sporty attire. However, he needn't have worried. She arrived with a turquoise t-shirt, denim shorts, tortoiseshell sunglasses and hair tied back. She had a lightweight, waterproof outfit, just in case. She also carried a dry bag which she explained was full of food and drinks.

Jussi noted her attire with approval and smiled at the dry bag.

"If nothing else, Selma, we won't go hungry or thirsty!"

"You never know. Let's see where this adventure takes us," she added with a wink.

They packed their kayaks, placing the bags into the storage ports and sealing them. The covers required some force to close, and just as Jussi was about to offer help, Selma closed them without assistance. Both crafts were sea kayaks, long, narrow and pointed. One was Jussi's usual yellow one, and there was a duplicate model, in white, for Selma.

They completed their preparation by stuffing their waterproofs and drinking bottles into the netting, laid across their vessels. They pulled their kayaks gently down the beach, entered the cockpits and gently pushed off into the sea.

Jussi was suitably impressed by how quickly Selma settled into her craft. The sun shone down, reflecting on the gently rippling water as they paddled away.

"How many times have you been kayaking?" asked Jussi suspiciously.

"Just a couple, but I enjoyed it and have always wanted to do it again."

They paddled side by side, heading out to sea, hugging the coast with their kayaks as they went.

They had been going non-stop for about an hour when they came across a small beach on a tiny island. They decided to stop there, enjoy a coffee and have a rest.

After pulling their kayaks onto the beach, they took some bags and walked to a dry sandy area. They laid out a picnic blanket and opened a flask of coffee, together with some fresh, warm pullas (cinnamon buns) that Selma had bought from a café that morning.

"This is perfect," Jussi exclaimed.

He took a bite of his pulla, drank a sip of coffee and relaxed against a rock. The sun was now beating down, but a cool breeze blew in from the sea.

"This feeling is exactly what I was hoping for. With the sun on my face and a relaxing day like this, with a handsome guy like you, what could be better?"

Jussi smiled his widest smile at her.

They finished their refreshments and lay down, naturally, side by side. They chatted idly for a while until their hands connected, and they rolled closer together and kissed.

After a while, they decided it was time to move. The couple had plans and a route to follow. They shoved off into the sea once more and paddled further into the widening straits.

Another half an hour later, they approached Jussi's planned destination. They circled the island, with him in front, until they came across the small river Jussi had located on the map - it was stunning. The sun was shining down on the water, which was almost still and the reeds stood to attention on each side, as they passed. Luckily, the mosquitos were kept at bay by the light breeze, and it was a delight to paddle gently downstream.

In a while, they came upon a small inlet that led from the

river. They paddled to the shore and decamped from the boats, taking their bags onto the grass. They found a large flat rock and set up their picnic feast. Jussi opened a small bottle of white wine, having carefully packed it in frozen packs. They each took a sip.

"Mmm, that's perfect. You certainly know how to prepare for a trip," Selma exclaimed. Then after a moment, she asked curiously, "What made you move to Helsinki?"

Jussi thought carefully for a moment.

"There were a few reasons: a promotion, a change of scene, and the end of a relationship."

"Ahh. I thought so. A break-up is often a reason to search for new pastures."

"Well, I guess several things happened at the same time. It wasn't exactly a break-up, more about becoming different people. Although, she also moved away for more drastic reasons," he replied, considering Heli for a moment.

"Can you tell me more?" Selma asked, with an intrigued expression on her face.

Jussi didn't really want to but decided to explain anyway. He told Selma about his old flame returning to Helsinki. Then, he described the events in and around Rauma, including the mystery of the 'Paintings of Rauma'. He went on to explain the time he had spent in Sweden and Singapore. Finally, he told the end of the story, when Heli had disappeared to the Caribbean and had last been seen in Cuba. He took his time and told the story in some detail, although he left out the more personal moments.

When he had finished, he gulped some wine from his glass and lay down. Selma had been sitting upright during his story, hanging onto his every word. Her mouth had dropped open at times, and occasionally gasped.

"Okay, that wasn't exactly what I expected to hear! What an incredible story."

"Yes, it is, isn't it?" he agreed, nodding his head gently.

"Do you still care for her?"

"Well, I do care for her, but I don't love her now if that's what you mean. There's also the fact that she's now a wanted criminal who was part of a gang that committed serious crimes - and I'm a Police Officer. So, no, I can't see us getting back together anytime soon," he smiled wistfully.

Selma moved a little closer.

"In that case, I can do this."

She rolled onto him and they began kissing again. This time they kissed with more urgency.

After some time, Jussi and Selma fell asleep in each other's arms, bathed in the warm sunshine, feeling drowsy from the wine.

❖ ❖ ❖

Jussi awoke after about an hour. The sun had cooled the day with the help of a few clouds. It was still daylight, being only late afternoon, but he felt it would soon be time to move on. It was also some distance to paddle back to the kayak centre.

Not wanting to wake Selma, he quietly took his camera and mobile phone. He walked up to the island's highest point, where he could see the sea once more, switched on his camera and began taking photographs of the area, nature and sky. As he did this, he found himself scanning the horizon for stolen boats as the content of the morning's messages arose in his mind once again However, he soon dismissed these thoughts and refocused his camera on the view in front of him.

Summer was his favourite season. At the start of the year, from its bleak wintry landscape, Finland slowly changed into a lush green abundance of trees and flowers. By June, the scene was completely different. All around him now, there were towering blue, white and purple delphiniums, dwarfing the heather and grasses. Daisies peaked through clumps of blueberry plants. The leaves of tall silver birches burst through the coniferous forest. Butterflies and dragonflies hovered among the sweet aromas, and seagulls called to each other across the breeze.

Jussi was so busy snapping away at the scene around him that he didn't notice a hand appear on his shoulder. He jumped a little.

"Hello, you," Selma smiled sleepily.

Jussi smiled and leaned in to kiss her. Then, they both took a seat on a large rock that overlooked the sea.

"What a view!" exclaimed Selma.

"Yes, it certainly is. I feel fortunate today."

The sea was calm, and the sky was spectacular. Dark clouds were slowly rolling in from the west. The sun was streaming in through gaps between the clouds, and Jussi took photographs of its reflection in the water. He turned to Selma while scanning the view.

"I think we should be going soon. Those dark clouds could mean rain, and kayaking in heavy rain for a couple of hours is no fun."

"I agree. Let's go," Semna replied.

They made their way back to the picnic spot, gathered their belongings and made their way back to the kayaks. After packing everything away securely, they put on their raincoats and pushed off into the sea once more.

The return journey was smooth at first, until a little before they landed. At that point, angry-looking clouds took over the sky, and the rain started. First, a drizzle began, and just as they were nearing the beach, the rain came down in sheets.

They paddled faster and faster as the waves became choppier. It was a real effort to complete their trip, and they were relieved to approach the shore, and more than happy to drag their kayaks onto the beach and run to the Kayak Centre for cover.

"Phew! We made it!" Jussi announced.

"Yep, the last ten minutes were getting interesting - it's a good feeling to be undercover again!"

"Oh, Hey!" Selma said, noting a sign on another building. "Should we have a sauna? I'm a bit cold now."

"Definitely!" Jussi replied.

There were separate Men's and ladies saunas within a single building. Before entering, they agreed to meet for coffee in half an hour.

After stripping off, Jussi sat in the sauna and threw some water on the stove. The hot steam took his breath for a moment, and he reflected on his day.

It had been a fantastic trip, and he had been delighted to spend it with Selma. He sat looking into the steam for a moment. He couldn't understand why his old flame Heli appeared in his thoughts once again, though. Perhaps it was Selma's question that had raised her in his mind? He did think about Heli from time to time, and on this occasion, he couldn't help but compare Selma to Heli. They were both adventurous, they both had incredible smiles, and he found life easy in their company. He found himself missing Heli now, and wondered how she was.

Is it normal to think about previous partners when I'm with someone new? he asked himself.

He dismissed Heli from his mind and filed her away. He focused back on Selma again. He would look forward to getting to know her better.

He threw another ladle of water onto the hot stones and nodded as someone else entered the sauna. They exchanged comments on the rain and talked a about kayaks and which were more suitable for such bad weather. After a few minutes, Jussi made his excuses and left.

After a quick shower, he found Selma already seated in the refreshments' area, nursing a hot mug of coffee.

"Hey, how was your sauna?" he inquired.

"Oh, it was amazing. I needed it after that rain. I feel so great," she replied. Then added, "Jussi, it's such a lousy day now, and I have my car here. Would you like to go somewhere else and have dinner together?"

"Sure, that would be great. Where did you have in mind?"

"Could I surprise you?"

"Why not?" he answered with a grin.

After they finished their steaming cups of coffee, they left and made for Selma's car. Jussi was impressed. It was an older car but in excellent condition. It was a Mazda, in bright yellow, with a convertible roof. After expressing his admiration, they drove off and arrived at an apartment block twenty minutes later.

"Nice area," Jussi exclaimed as they walked to the building. "Your place?" he asked.

"You guessed it," she grinned. "Come on, let's go inside, and I can show you around."

They only just managed to get through the door before they began pulling frantically at one anothers' clothes. Within a few seconds, they were both naked. They made love for some time, and afterwards, Jussi pulled Selma close and held her.

◆ ◆ ◆

They spent a delightful evening chatting with one other over an enormous salad they prepared together.

After the light dinner and a couple of glasses of wine, they found themselves back in bed again. It was 11.15 pm before Jussi kissed Selma goodnight and left her apartment. He jumped into the taxi he had called, and within thirty minutes, was back inside his apartment downtown.

It had been a great day, the best one he could remember, at least since the last time he had seen Selma.

Jussi rolled into bed at midnight and thought about her, then Heli, and then Selma again, before he rolled over and finally fell asleep.

THE PHOTOGRAPH

The following morning, Jussi arose from bed a little later. His working day would begin at 10 am, and the task force meeting would not start until 11 am. This gave him time to relax over coffee, together with his laptop.

He sat flicking through the photographs he had taken the day before. He had some excellent shots of the coast and laughed when he found one of Selma in the kayak, smiling at him with that mischievous smile of hers. He looked at it and wondered if, at that point, she had already planned that the day would end at her apartment. He smiled again as his thoughts wandered.

He continued scanning through the photographs on his screen and selected various pictures to retain and others to delete. Then he filed them away. As he did so, he flicked through some of the ones from his previous trip, deleting a couple that had been super-ceded in quality by newer ones. He stopped at a particular photograph and eyed it curiously.

"That's the boat!" he exclaimed in surprise.

He continued looking at the picture and increased the size of the screen to gain a better view. Now he could see it unquestionably. He remembered it from the case file. It was the boat that had been found with the body inside. At the point he had taken the picture, it was sitting safely in its berth. He checked the date and time of the picture, which proved he had taken it during his solo kayaking trip the previous Tuesday evening. Jussi sat back to think. He wondered why the boat had been stolen and where it had been, left with only a body on board.

He checked more photographs of the area and noted the same boat on some of those too. He could track it at different dates and times, safely moored at the same point. It seemed to Jussi that he enjoyed shooting the same scenes, as he had snapped them every time he had paddled past in the kayak. Then he came across another photograph, taken on his return journey.

"So, you were there at 10.02 pm but had been stolen before 10.38 pm. Now, where did you go then?" he asked into thin air.

He thought about the boat and how close it was found to the harbour. He thought about the other thefts. He remembered the one that had been reported as it was in the process of being stolen. That one also seemed to have disappeared quickly and couldn't have gone that far.

Jussi placed the photographs in a separate folder and emailed them to his police email address. He would bring those up in the meeting that morning, but now he needed to move, so he closed his laptop and got himself ready for work.

Before leaving, he sent a short text to Selma:

Thank you for such a great day yesterday. Looking forward to the next time. Jussi.

◆ ◆ ◆

Following his usual commute, Jussi arrived at the station. After a brief chat about life with Toni, one of the uniformed officers, he went to his desk. He downloaded the photographs from his email account and sent them to print. Meanwhile, he read the information about the boat he had seen.

From the register, it was clear it was seldom used. In fact, it had probably only been on the water for a few good weather weekends each year. He deduced it had been stolen in the short period he had identified, then taken elsewhere to be hidden. That place could've been where the unknown victim had been shot on board or possibly somewhere else first. From the forensics report, it seemed likely to be the former.

Suddenly a hand appeared on his shoulder.

"Well, how did your weekend go?"

Jussi looked up and saw Tapio rubbing his hands with a sparkle in his eye.

"Well, that would be between the lady and me," he replied with a broad smile on his face.

"Okay, say no more," Tapio remarked, tapping his nose, his face carrying an even wider smile.

Jussi shook his head in mock despair and changed the subject before he started to turn crimson.

"Hey Tapsa, I found this photograph of the stolen boat from my collection of photos taken from my kayak - look."

They both leaned in, and Jussi explained his theory.

"I think you're right," Tapio agreed. "These boats are not being taken far away, at least not at first. We need to start searching the coast and the islands."

"Exactly," said Jussi. "We could start looking at possible landing locations, or places where a boat could be concealed, maybe within an hour of the harbour?"

Tapio disappeared and returned with a large-scale map. He beckoned to Jussi and spread it out across the large meeting table in the corner of the room. Jussi took a ruler and a marker pen, and with it, he measured an arc from the harbour to an estimate of an hour away. Then, they started to mark possible locations where a boat could be taken and hidden. They also circled those points where a nearby road or river could be utilised to transport the boats away from a temporary hiding place. When they finished, the plan looked reasonable enough, so they took it to the Detective Sergeant's office.

Pekka eyed the map and waited patiently while Jussi explained the theory, supported by Tapio.

"Well, it's just a theory but could be worth a look. These boats are of high value and the thefts are stacking up. I don't want the bodies to start doing the same either."

Jussi and Tapio exchanged glances and thanked Pekka for his time. They were soon driving towards Helsinki to meet a representative from the Police Marine Unit, whom they had engaged to help them.

After parking, the two detectives climbed aboard the police launch. It was a small but powerful vessel with two huge outboard motors at the stern.

"Wow, I wonder what this boat will do when these engines are opened up to full throttle?" Jussi asked.

Tapio nodded. He didn't want to find out. this was not in his comfort zone. He liked boats and was currently looking for one, but not quite as fast as this one might go - way too much movement for him. As the vessel glided away into the sea proper, a noticeable swell began, so he sat down and concentrated on the horizon.

Meanwhile, Jussi was chatting to the driver, Salli, a bright, young and cheery officer with a great sense of humour. They enjoyed their conversation and the time passed quickly.

Shortly afterwards, they arrived at the first destination and alighted to check for possible clues. There were far too many large rocks and overhanging trees, so they abandoned it and moved on to the next location. This one was a gravel beach that had possibilities. They jumped ashore to inspect it and check for places where a trailer could have been brought. This one was too steep around the beach, though. It would be impossible to move anything from there, and it also was too exposed to hide anything.

They stopped and drank a coffee, trying to help Tapio feel better before moving on to the following place. This one was a barren island made up of enormous rocks. There was a channel of water separating it from the mainland. This one didn't seem practical either, so they abandoned it.

The detectives spent some time investigating other islands, nooks and crannies of the coastline around Helsinki. Jussi had to admit to himself that it was quite an enjoyable way to spend a day. However, in the circumstances, Tapio disagreed.

As the afternoon wore on, it seemed the plan was unlikely to yield any success despite it being a good idea. They decided to press on and continue to the last couple of places they had marked on the map. This was more out of due diligence rather than anything else.

An hour later, these possibilities had proved fruitless and they finished their task, empty-handed of any new leads.

"Well, at least it has given us more of a feeling for the scene of the crime," Jussi remarked as they turned to head back towards the harbour. He continued, "We know they left in this general direction but now understand the challenges they would face trying to escape."

"Yes, despite the long coastline, there are very few places where you could hide or remove a boat without it being in plain sight," replied Tapio.

"Yes, you're right, Tapsa. Perhaps that's the next step. Rather than trying to find a hidden escape route, let's start to look at the public places where they could've casually removed a boat from the water. I wonder how many of them have CCTV cameras or other security?"

When they arrived at the dock, they thanked Salli, their host, returned to their car and headed back to the station. They could have clocked off at that point but were feeling some pressure from recent discussions. Instead, they decided to do some desktop research and prepare for the following day.

On their return to the station, they sat at their desks and began to study the maps once more. They both spent time with their computers, checking addresses and surveying potential sites to visit.

After a couple of hours, as it turned 7 pm, they decided to finish for the day. They had plotted more places to visit, plus a list of company addresses and telephone numbers to check. Also, during the next day, they would try and locate some video footage, witnesses or any other information to help them track down the thieves. They had discussed that this would probably take them the whole week, and there would be more to check afterwards, so they sent a request for some uniform support. They now had a clear plan of action.

"Let's call it a day?" suggested Jussi.

"Definitely," agreed Tapio. "I'll pick up a car and collect you from your apartment tomorrow. It doesn't make sense for you to come here first."

"Perfect, thanks, Tapsa," Jussi agreed. "See you tomorrow."

Jussi returned home. He cooked some simple noodles and chicken in a wok for his dinner, with a dash of soy sauce. He sat and ate while flicking through his phone, reading various personal messages and emails. He noted there had been no reply from Selma but hoped she would answer soon. He had to admit to thinking about her several times that day and was a little unnerved at how much she had interrupted his thoughts.

After eating, he settled down on his sofa to look at more photographs. His visit to Selma's apartment, with its warm and welcoming interior, had made him think about how bare his own place looked. If he invited Selma here, he should probably do something to impress her.

He decided that one of those things would be to decorate one of the walls with his photographs. He considered the wall and decided to buy some black, rectangular picture frames in which to display his best images. He wanted the space to look a little more designed, so he chose a variety of sizes. He would buy them tomorrow if he had time.

After opening his laptop, He flicked through the folders and marked different photographs as possibilities. After an hour and a half, he had designated thirty pictures. He decided he couldn't buy so many frames and forced himself to narrow it down to a selection of twelve images for twelve frames.

As he began to look more carefully, he studied the picture containing the suspect vessel once more. He started to look at more photographs containing boats. He idly flicked through them, one by one and stopped at one of them. He looked carefully at a particular shot and increased the magnification to view it with more visible detail.

The picture was from another of his kayak excursions and clearly showed a man driving a boat out to sea. There was nothing suspicious, but it provoked a thought in Jussi's mind.

What if they didn't hide them or take them out of the water on the coast? What if they just drove straight out to sea? Is that how they can disappear so fast? These boats are strong enough. Could they even steer them to another country?

Jussi dismissed the idea. These were not long-distance vessels, and they wouldn't survive the Baltic Sea. He pondered his thoughts for a moment longer and decided their current course of action was still a good one. Tomorrow and the next day would involve some considerable leg-work. Still, if nothing else, it would alert boat owners and marine management companies to monitor activity or install proper security. At least they could reduce the opportunity for further crime.

DISAPPEARING ACT

Samuli checked his watch: it was approaching 1 am. He looked at Hemmo, who was busy demolishing a sandwich. He was getting tired. They had been sitting there for almost an hour, and he was itching to get going. If they did the job soon and moved quickly, he could be at home, sleeping in bed, within a couple of hours.

The car was parked across the road from a small marina, close to some offices. It was not their car. It had been procured specifically for the purpose. Samuli was aware of the increased police activity around the main harbour and decided it was time they began to work some of the smaller marinas. This particular one had been at the top of his list. Due to nearby office blocks, he preferred to use a stolen car to ensure security cameras didn't pick them up. They also disguised themselves, dressed from head to toe in black, carrying balaclavas for when they might be exposed.

They waited for another ten minutes until a slightly inebriated younger couple meandered past the car and around the corner. Samuli did his best to wait patiently.

"Let's go," directed Hemmo.

The two thieves put on their balaclavas and walked down the street. They were only a minute from the water's edge and were on the dock and onto their selected boat quickly and easily. Samuli struggled under the dashboard for a couple of minutes, and then the engine fired into life. Hemmo released the dock lines, and they gently eased away into the night. An easy job this time.

Hemmo opened the throttle a little, and they continued at medium speed for around thirty minutes. They wanted to keep moving but keep the noise to a minimum. They arrived at the open sea and fired up the engines to the maximum. They always chose powerful boats, and this one was no exception. It roared as it sped away into the distance and away from Helsinki. The speed, wind and noise gave no opportunity to talk about anything, so the thieves sat looking determinedly ahead.

Hemmo studied the satellite navigation device they had brought with them. After hot-wiring the ignition and disabling the GPS and radar, they usually had no means of navigation, so they always carried their own. He noted they were on target, and his gaze swopped between the horizon and the screen. Despite it being summer and the boat having a canopy, it was chilly, so they buttoned up their jackets.

After another half an hour, they were relieved to near their destination. Hemmo nodded at Samuli, and they cut the engine. Samuli opened their bag and took out a small but powerful beacon. He switched it on, and its light penetrated the night. They waited for a few minutes, and faint lights appeared ahead. Samuli reached for his Glock handgun, stashed in his jacket. He was naturally careful, and the lights could belong to a coastguard or police patrol. His suspicions were unfounded, though. After flashing their lights three times as a signal, a larger vessel, a fishing boat, drew up alongside.

A line was cast to their smaller craft, and a ladder dropped from the side of the fishing vessel. The men secured the ropes and climbed on board.

"Labkavar!" (Good Evening) shouted Edgars, in Latvian, appearing at the top of the ladder, flanked by two men.

"Paldies," (Thank You) replied Hemmo as he made his way over the side rail and onto the deck.

"Everything okay with this one? Any problems tonight?" asked Edgars.

"Everything went smoothly. She's a fine boat," answered Hemmo, as Samuli arrived on board beside him.

"Okay, let's get it on board," Edgars instructed his crew.

One of the men climbed down onto the stolen boat, while another operated a control box. At his command, a crane and pulley system moved slowly over the fishing vessel's side and downwards. The man on the stolen boat took hold of various cables and attached them at multiple points. When he had secured it, he climbed back up the ladder and waited. The crane pulled the boat from the water, and the man on the ladder moved another part of the hanging crane underneath it. He then climbed back onto the fishing vessel and attached the cables to a thick chain. When it was sufficiently secured, the craft was raised entirely out of the water and swung on deck. All hands helped to guide it over the open hold, and their bounty was lowered safely inside.

Within twenty minutes, the boat had been raised from the water and safely hidden in the hold. The men then placed iron grids onto slots above it and carefully stacked fishing crates across them. Now it had disappeared entirely from view, and it was time for them to get underway.

Most fishing vessels in the area, if successful, could expect to make a few thousand euros per trip. This one had caught a boat worth around 80,000€ which would quickly sell on the Russian Black Market. After a few adjustments to conceal its origin, it would sell for around 60,000€. For their part, Hemmo and Samuli would receive a bounty of 10,000€ to be split equally between them.

The fishing boat started its engines, and the throbbing of its large engine slowly swung the boat around. After turning, it began to make its way towards its destination. The two Finnish thieves knew the route well due to regular trips with their Latvian partners-in-crime. They were headed to a small inlet near Jurmala, the seaside resort of Latvia.

After the voyage, they would receive a lift in a car to Riga and catch a train from the central station to Tallinn, Estonia. From there, they would return to Helsinki via one of the ferries that regularly ran between the two countries. It was a long haul but judged to be safer than returning by any other means to Finland.

They neared the coast of Latvia, and the team donned their disguises. If they were boarded by the coastguard or customs, then they would look the part. They chugged past Jurmala, visible in the distance and continued to a small privately-owned harbour about a kilometre down the coast.

It didn't take long for them to arrive. They glided into their sanctuary, after which they stopped and dropped anchor.

The gang went through the same process with the stolen boat, only in reverse. They carefully hoisted the boat up, swung it across and placed it down into the sea, with one of Edgars' men on board. The engines were started, and it was driven into a large boathouse.

Within a few minutes, the doors were closed as if the vessel had never been there. Edgars looked at the Finns and nodded.

"Good. Another one in progress. When can we expect the next?"

Hemmo replied, "It may be a short while. We've noticed an increased police presence around the main harbour, so we'll have to spend more time changing places to look for targets. If we are seen too often or videoed on security cameras, we may have some problems."

"Well, this boat isn't going to make us millionaires. It will just pay some costs. It takes a lot of time to convert these boats to something we can sell without immediately being recognised. We need more boats and, if possible, more expensive ones."

"How much demand do you have now?" asked Hemmo.

"Practically unlimited. There are plenty of Russians who are happy to pay for a boat like this, provided it is cleaned of its former existence, but they still want a good deal."

"Well, let's see what we can do," Hemmo replied.

"See that you do that," Edgars said.

Samuli regarded the Latvian with a frown. He wasn't impressed that they seemed to have transitioned from being partners to being treated like the hired help.

Edgars caught the expression and smiled, "Don't worry Samuli, one day you will be a happy and a rich man. Much better than being a dead one like our other Latvian friend eh?"

Samuli grunted.

A small boat arrived to take Hemmo and Samuli to shore, continuing their onward journey. The fishing vessel would now return to a dock near Jurmala. When not being used for this purpose, it was catching fish, completing its disguise. Now that the next stolen boat had arrived in Latvia, the next stage in its life would begin.

THE WAVES OF HELSINKI

SHOTS FIRED

"Buzzz."

The alarm rang out and Jussi opened his eyes. He picked up his phone and checked for messages. There was one message from the station that caught his interest: another boat had been taken overnight.

Jussi got out of bed and dressed. He grabbed a bowl, made some muesli and stood eating it. He had dreamt that night, and unusually for him, he could remember some of it. The dream had featured his former girlfriend, Heli.

In the beginning, they had both been in Cuba. They were managing a beach bar and suddenly had to run away, although he couldn't remember from what. He was annoyed with himself for dreaming about Heli. He had just met a terrific new girl who seemed to be fond of him, and could see it being a successful relationship - so why couldn't he forget about Heli and erase her from his mind?

He dismissed these thoughts as best he could, determined to concentrate on the case at hand. He could see the task force being expanded and his role potentially diminishing, so he had to be seen as active and also as productive as possible; he was determined to stand out to the senior officers. He finished his cereal, quickly downed a coffee and left his apartment to wait outside for Tapio to arrive.

◆ ◆ ◆

At the station, the Detective Inspector had received another call. This one was from the Chief Inspector of Police. It had not been pleasant due to a long discussion about the stolen boats and the murder. The chief demanded to know what progress was being made. The conversation had ended in a direct order to get the problem solved without delay. As is often the case with this kind of call, the content was passed down the line. In this case, the unlucky recipient was Tapio.

The call finished just as Tapio's car drew up by Jussi's apartment building, opposite the small park on Bulevardi Avenue. Jussi crossed the street and stepped inside. As he did so, he saw Tapio's face.

"You were lucky you missed that phone call!" he said, grimacing.

"What phone call?" Jussi answered.

"The Inspector just called me. He isn't thrilled about our progress. The task force is being expanded as a result, but only by two part-time officers, as most resources are needed for the midsummer events over the next few weeks. Whatever the case, we need to show some progress. Let's get this show on the road."

Tapio drove off towards Lautasaari, one of the small connecting islands of Helsinki. Lautasaari has a few small harbours, usually full of boats in the summer and today was no exception.

The detectives arrived and decamped at the main dock. They walked around the area and chatted to a few boat owners about to set off for a day on the sea. The site was well-covered by CCTV cameras, and there had been no theft from there as yet.

Afterwards, they sat in the small carpark. Tapio monitored the area whilst Jussi worked on his laptop and pulled up the list of boat owners registered there. He wrote an email to alert them of the situation and advised them to consider special trackers. These trackers were often found on larger boats but not usually fitted to smaller crafts.

When they had sent the messages, they moved to the next location to repeat the process. They would receive a resource to help them in the office soon. At least then, these administrative tasks could be done by someone else while they concentrated upon more productive activities.

They spent the rest of the day checking further small harbours, talking to boat-owners, harbour masters, residents and monitoring the area by just walking around. They were pleased to meet uniformed officers in some locations, having been instructed to show a visible presence.

At lunchtime, they visited a local hamburger kiosk, and as it was a sunny day, they ate them sitting by the water.

"Well, no sign of a breakthrough yet," muttered Jussi.

"No, not yet," replied Tapio, shaking his head.

Tapio had a habit of raising his eyebrows every time he said something. This had amused Jussi at first, and he had found himself deliberately trying to ignore it - meaning he had inadvertently ended up staring instead. Over time, he had developed a strategy of looking at Tapio's mouth or ear rather than his eyebrows, and this seemed to be working so far.

Jussi took the last bite of his burger. It was one of those cheap ones from a small kiosk, the kind that people usually eat late at night after a few beers, but it tasted good at that moment. They washed the burgers down with an ice-cold can of cola each.

"Okay, ready to go?" enquired Jussi.

Tapio indicated that he was, and they returned to the car. They were gradually ticking off their list, but it would still take some days, even with the support they had begun to receive from the office. As Tapio started the engine, a call came through on the radio.

"There have been shots fired at the Seurasaari Marina, and a boat has been stolen. One person has been injured. There is a danger to public safety, and all officers in the area should respond."

The two detectives looked at each other, and Tapio gunned the car as they responded to the message. As they drove, Jussi removed their guns from the secure glove compartment and checked them while Tapio navigated rapidly towards the scene, lights flashing and siren blaring.

The traffic was light, so they arrived at the marina in less than fifteen minutes. They pulled up by the curb and left the car, moving quickly towards the dock. They could already see a crowd of people, so they quickly made for them.

On arrival, they pushed their way through and found they were the first to arrive. One person was kneeling, pressing some clothing against a man lying on the ground. Tapio knelt to help him.

"Jussi, I'll assist here, find out where the shooter has gone."

Jussi immediately questioned the crowd, "Where did the shooter go?"

"Over there," a young man replied and pointed. "I saw some of what happened. A guy shot him and then drove a boat away with someone else."

Jussi ran towards the space where the boat had been. He looked out to sea but couldn't see anything. He saw a man standing in a launch at the end of the dock and ran over.

"Can we use your boat?" he asked.

"Well, yes, I suppose so. Do I drive it?" the man answered.

"Yes, please," Jussi said, jumping aboard.

He looked back and saw no sign of Tapio, who would no doubt wait until the ambulance had arrived and then secure the scene with uniformed officers.

"Let's go!" directed Jussi.

The man nodded, powered up the bow thrusters, and the boat lunged forward, causing Jussi to sit down rather quickly. It seemed that he had chosen the right boat as it sped along the crests of the waves out of the harbour. Jussi pointed in the direction of the open sea, and the man obliged, pointing the stern to the horizon. He thought they might have a chance of catching up with the perpetrators, but was concerned about having a member of the public with him. He decided that if they caught up with the thieves, they would remain at a safe distance and direct other police resources to their location.

They passed an assortment of different vessels but nothing that appeared to contain the two suspects. He radioed back and made contact with the coastguard, who were already scanning the area. A helicopter had also been dispatched and would be in the area within minutes.

"What's your name?" Jussi asked the owner of his borrowed boat.

"Simo," the man replied.

"Thanks for your help, Simo," he shouted over the noise of the engines. "It seems we may be too late. However, I'd still like to circle the area and see if the boat turns up anywhere. The coastguard boat will go east, so let's go west around the islands. We're looking for a medium-sized, black boat, so please shout if you see one."

Simo nodded and turned the boat southwest, away from the coast, as Jussi scanned the area for boats that would fit the description. Simo handed Jussi a pair of binoculars, which he accepted gratefully and immediately put to work.

They spent another hour and a half searching the area, but it was to no avail. The communications from the other boats informed Jussi that the craft had apparently disappeared into thin air.

He asked Simo to return to the harbour, and within an hour, they were back in the boat's original berth. Jussi thanked him.

"No problem," replied Simo. "This was the most exciting trip I've had in a long time."

Jussi smiled and returned to the scene of the shooting. By this time, there were several police vehicles parked there. Yellow tape cordoned off much of the area. The crowd had been dispersed, and the victim had been taken to hospital. The man involved had received a bullet wound, but luckily, it was not too severe, and he was expected to fully recover.

Jussi met up with Tapio again.

"What happened here, Tapsa?"

Tapio related the events that had occurred since Jussi had disappeared out to sea. Jussi reciprocated with the story of his search for the perpetrators.

"So, where are they going?" Jussi asked Tapio. "How can they just disappear like that every time?"

"Well, they seem to be getting more desperate. This theft was in broad daylight, and the suspects even shot someone. I guess we knew they were capable of that anyway, if the dead body found in the boat was their handiwork. They're probably always armed and dangerous on these raids. It seems as if we have pirates in Helsinki now!"

After some discussion and further questioning of the

witnesses, they were informed that the injured man was the boat's owner and undoubtedly the best lead they had now.

They drove to the hospital, and Jussi noted two text messages from Selma. Although he had been happy to receive them, it wasn't a good time to respond - his head was elsewhere. He returned the phone to his pocket and resolved to call her later that day.

On arrival at the hospital, they had to wait for some time. The victim had been taken into surgery, and the Doctor was strict about the recovery time.

A short while later, Jussi and Tapio were pleased to learn that the man had gone through surgery without issue. They would be allowed to see him for a short time but only after three hours. So, they waited.

◆ ◆ ◆

The stolen boat was cutting through the waves and approaching the meeting point, allowing conversation to take place.

"That was close," Samuli commented to Hemmo, while simultaneously heaving a deep sigh.

Hemmo looked at Samuli and shook his head as he was thinking. They had taken a considerable risk this time. They had been fortunate, but the chaos they had caused might result in problems further down the line. As they approached the fishing boat, Edgars appeared from the cabin.

He sneered, "When I ask you to bring me another boat, I don't mean to bring me a whole load of trouble as well. I've been listening to the news. This mess could put coastguards on the alert across the whole region."

"We've made more money for you. What do you care?"

answered Samuli.

Edgars glared at him and replied, "Because I want to get home in one piece. What you did today may have jeopardised the whole operation."

"Edgars, you cannot push for more boats in one moment and then complain about the consequences in the next. We did what we had to do! Let's give it a week to calm down, and it will all blow over. There are plenty more boats we can find for you, and this little one will be worth a nice profit for all of us."

"Just make sure the next one causes less noise," Edgars commented as he walked back towards the cabin.

The boat got underway, and the engines chugged their way back across the sea, in the direction of Latvia.

◆ ◆ ◆

At the hospital, Jussi and Tapio were anxiously awaiting the opportunity to interview the shooting victim. Finally, a nurse appeared and gestured that they enter the private room where he was recovering.

The man's name was Frederik Jacobsen. He was a Dane that worked in one of the big accounting firms and kept his boat in a harbour near his office. This provided him with the ability to quickly slip away on evening cruises, straight after work in the summer.

When the detectives entered the room, they observed that he looked well enough, except for his arm and chest being bandaged. The Doctor informed them that the bullet had gone straight through the soft tissue of his arm and passed directly through the side of his chest. Fortunately, the projectile had not hit anything else on its way.

The Detectives introduced themselves and, as time was

short, got straight down to business.

"Did you get a good look at the person who shot you? Or at the second individual?" Jussi asked.

"I saw the person who shot me but just for a moment. It all happened so quickly," the witness answered.

"What did he look like?" Tapio asked.

There followed a vague description that painted an elementary profile of the shooter. Apparently, he had not seen the second man at all, as he had his back to him.

If Hemmo had been listening, he would have been concerned to hear himself described, although not in any great detail.

Tapio informed Frederik that an artist would visit him to draw an impression of the man. Jussi and Tapio thanked him and turned to leave. Unfortunately, they hadn't gleaned any helpful information, over and above what they had received from other witnesses.

"Oh, there is one more thing that may help track the boat," Frederik commented.

"Yes?" Jussi asked.

"The boat has a special anti-theft tracker. I had it fitted when I bought the new boat. I thought it was a bit pointless afterwards, as nobody steals anything here, but now it may prove useful."

Jussi and Tapio looked at each other with some hope.

"So, how exactly does it work?" Jussi asked, his attention grabbed once more.

❖ ❖ ❖

Selma finished her day at the office. She had planned to go to the gym, but now something was bothering her. She found it challenging to work out when something was on her mind.

She had messaged Jussi twice that day and was prepared to send a third but decided it would look too eager. She didn't want to appear desperate to see him again. In fact, she wasn't desperate to see him at all but would have been pleased for him to communicate somehow. She was also keen to set a date in the diary for the next time they would meet. Deep in thought, she walked towards the station, a little upset and annoyed.

"Oh, screw that," she uttered under her breath.

She wasn't going to let this guy get under her skin. She had been here before. She turned around and headed back to the street where her gym was located. She would work out and then go and grab some sushi at her favourite place.

Within fifteen minutes, Selma was running on the treadmill, running somewhere that only she knew.

IN RIGA

Hemmo and Samuli boarded the bus to Tallinn. They took their seats, stretched out and prepared for the journey. It would take several hours to reach the Estonian capital, and they each had their selection of snacks, drinks and entertainment, with which to pass the time. The bus was due to arrive later in the evening.

They had discussed the issues in Helsinki and decided that the best plan was to lie low in Tallinn for a couple of days. To this end, they had booked themselves into a small hotel in the old quarter of town. A couple of days of eating, drinking and relaxing would shake off any remaining nerves.

Shortly after departing, Hemmo's mobile phone rang, it was Edgars.

"We have another problem. We found a tracking device on the boat. Instead of destroying it, we took it further down the coast and dropped it into the sea near Ventspils. That way, they won't be able to trace us so easily."

"So, what do we do now?" asked Hemmo.

"Do as planned. Lie low somewhere, and we'll take care of it. I doubt if anything will happen, but we'll need to suspend things for a week to be sure. We'll get rid of this boat as soon as possible, and I'll call you when it's time to move - you really screwed things up this time," added Edgars as he ended the call.

Samuli eyed Hemmo expectantly. When he was told the

news, he shook his head in response. They both sat back in their seats and reclined.

"Perhaps we should extend this trip?" Hemmo asked.

Samuli grunted in agreement and put his headphones back on as the bus continued.

◆ ◆ ◆

Jussi's ex-girlfriend, Heli, was in Cuba.

Today, she was walking along the beach barefoot. She felt the grains of sand slip through her toes as she did so. She smiled as she looked up at the horizon - it would be another hot day. She had dressed in a simple white linen dress, carefully chosen to display her deliciously warm bronze tan. She wore her hair tied back in her original hair colour of auburn, contrasting with the locally-made jewellery of stones and shells around her neck, wrist and ankles.

Thinking of breakfast, she stopped at a small café and ordered a cortado with a croissant. The coffee came with a small glass of ice-cold water which she drank immediately. She spoke in Spanish, now that her command of the language was growing, and she felt able to survive in most places in Cuba with it. She had hired a local teacher, who taught her twice per week. If this was her home, she wanted to be able to communicate and blend in as much as possible.

Heli had arrived in Cuba a few months before. She initially enjoyed staying in different hotels but then decided to remain and put down more permanent roots. This was mostly because she had read about the ongoing international hunt for her, following the crimes related to 'The Paintings of Rauma' case. She knew she could never return to Finland again.

She had been hard at work making arrangements for a

new life. Firstly, she went to the immigration ministry, and arranged to set up a company and invest money in Cuba. This had expedited her papers to remain. Following this, a quick but significant decision had been to purchase a small hotel on the coast.

With the help of the hotel's general manager, she started to develop it and soon after re-launched the resort as an eco-tourist destination. She used her marketing expertise to brand the resort and attracted some local private investment to expand. She had decided to live on the premises and converted one of the beach cottages for herself. Everything seemed to be working out well, with one exception: she was missing Jussi.

Heli had been so busy of late that there had been no real time to do anything about that particular matter. As she was now feeling safe and secure on the island, she felt more comfortable about romantic entanglements, provided they were brief. However, this week, more than ever, Jussi had been on her mind.

After finishing breakfast, she continued walking along the beach until she approached her property. She sat down on a favourite rock, removed her mobile phone and dialled Jussi's number.

"Hey, Jussi here," he answered.

"Hey, Jussi," Heli replied

"Just a moment."

There were muffled voices as his hand covered the mouthpiece.

"Heli? Where are you? Are you alright?" he asked, in some amazement to have received her call.

"Yes, I'm fine, Jussi. How are you?" she answered.

"Well, things are fine here as usual. I'm in Helsinki now. Remember that weekend when we were here?" he asked, when he was safely in a corridor.

Heli looked down as she pushed her toes into the sand.

"Yes, I do. Very well. It feels like a long time ago now."

"Are you safe? Are you still in Cuba?"

"Yes, and I'm living here now, Jussi. I have my own business, a cottage on the beach, and well, now I'm settled. I thought I'd call you and say hello. Perhaps even invite you to Cuba?"

"Oh yes, that would look good, wouldn't it? I can see the newspaper headlines now: Detective visits International Fugitive."

"Well, anyway, who knows, maybe one day. What do you think?"

"I think the best idea for you is to stay far away. Disappear Heli, just disappear."

Heli looked downwards at her feet, which were digging further into the sand as they spoke.

"Yes, Jussi. You're probably right. Goodbye. Take care."

"Good bye Heli. You take care too. Let's talk again."

Jussi waited until the call ended with a click and looked up at the ceiling.

That was a call he hadn't expected to receive. He walked to the window and looked outside, with all kinds of thoughts going through his mind. He shook his head and pushed her out of his mind as he returned to the matter in-hand, walking back into the meeting room where they had been discussing the next steps of the task force. The GPS tracker had been a real benefit and they were looking forward to the next step of the investigation.

Thank goodness they don't know who I was speaking to, thought Jussi.

During the meeting, Tapio revealed that he had obtained permission for Jussi to visit Latvia for two days, with a possible two day extension if the evidence justified it; Jussi was to travel to Riga.

◆ ◆ ◆

Jussi arrived home that evening, removed his shoes, took off his coat, walked into his apartment and flopped down onto the sofa. He sat there for a few moments, once again pondering the phone call out of the blue from Heli. He felt her around him again and that old feelings had resurfaced.

His thoughts turned to Selma. He realized that between everything that had happened, plus the call from Heli, he had forgotten to reply to her messages. He thought about her for a little longer. He really liked her. He recalled their day on the waves, in the kayaks. That had definitely been one of the best days he could remember, at least since Heli had been around. He resolved to improve at handling relationships and decided to call her immediately.

"Moi," answered Selma, recognising the number on the display.

Jussi could tell that her voice was not entirely happy to hear from him, or at least that was how it had been designed to be heard.

"Moi Selma, how are you?" he asked.

"I'm fine, thank you," she answered.

Yes, there was definitely a coolness in her voice.

"Sorry, I haven't had an opportunity to reply to your

messages. The case has been so busy in the last couple of days."

"No problem Jussi. I've been quite busy myself. I hope everything is going fine at work?"

"Yes, it is. Well, at least we have some leads to follow now," he replied. And then continued, "Hey, should we arrange to meet?"

"Maybe. I have a free day the day after tomorrow. Perhaps we could meet for lunch?" she offered.

"Ah! I have to go to Riga for a couple of days. How about at the weekend?"

"Sorry Jussi, I'm away in Tampere then, with some of my old friends."

"Okay. How is your next week?" he pressed.

After some discussions, they settled on the following Tuesday evening. He offered to take her for something different. She had accepted. He wasn't sure what that date would involve at this stage, but he could think about that later. He also decided to send her a couple of texts whilst he was away. He would try and manage this situation a little better.

That evening, he cooked a simple meal of noodles and soy sauce with some added tuna from a can, together with a couple of tomatoes he had found in the fridge. He decided he would have to go shopping again to refill his fresh food supplies, but that would have to wait until he returned from his trip. Then he set about packing.

Riga? He liked that city. Although it was geographically close, he hadn't been there for a while, not since he had visited a long time ago with his parents. He took his case and packed some casual clothes and a spare jacket.

It should be warm there now, he thought, but decided to add a raincoat just in case.

The flight would leave early in the morning. The plan was to meet the local police first and visit some possible locations, as identified by the GPS data. Perhaps Latvia would hold the answer to the mystery of the boat thefts and the murder?

Jussi turned in early to get some sleep.

◆ ◆ ◆

The alarm clock on Jussi's mobile phone went off at 5 am. He turned it off and got out of bed. It was getting near to midsummer now, and outside was brighter than ever. The Finnish Juhannus celebrations would take place in less than two weeks. He still hadn't planned what he would do, but for now, he had more pressing things to think about.

After his usual light breakfast of muesli and coffee, he set off for the airport. He walked to the central station and caught a direct train. In less than 30 minutes, he arrived at the terminal. He had packed light, as he always did, so there was no need to check a bag. He printed his boarding pass, underwent security, made his way to the gate and bought a cappuccino from the small café. Then he sat down and waited.

The plane arrived on time, and he was soon sitting on board. The flight would only take around an hour, and with nobody sitting adjacent, he decided to use the time to review the case notes.

The most recently stolen boat, involving the shooting incident, had been tracked in several places. It was not a particularly hi-tech unit and couldn't follow the journey undertaken; however, it could accurately pinpoint the current location. The police had been able to take the reading a few times since they had been notified of the tracking device. They had records of it being near the coast in several places, between Jurmula and Ventspils.

Communication between the Finnish and Latvian authorities had already resulted in a raid at Ventspils docks. However, on inspection the boat had been nowhere to be seen. Of course, they considered it could have been a false trail, or the device could have been removed in Ventspils, and the vessel moved elsewhere.

The purpose of Jussi's trip was to brief the Latvian police in detail, engage them in a joint approach and investigate any potential leads they might have. Sometimes, known criminals are the people to talk to first and the local police would be invaluable in this regard.

Jussi spent the remainder of the flight reading about the events to date and in particular, familiarising himself with the other stolen boats.

◆ ◆ ◆

Jussi arrived at the airport in Riga on time and was met by Janis, a young, smartly dressed Latvian detective. Jussi took a liking to him almost immediately as they talked on their way to the police station in Riga. Janis would be Jussi's buddy there and his link to the Latvian police.

On arrival at the station, they met two other detectives, named Ilgvars and Andris. Ilgvars was the chief detective, and Andris was his assistant.

"Good Morning Detective Alhonen," Ilgvars greeted Jussi.

"Please, call me Jussi. It's a pleasure to meet you."

After the introductions, which also involved coffee and pastries, Jussi took them through the case to date. There had been few such boat thefts in Latvia; however, they were aware of smuggling networks involved in the robbery and transfer of stolen goods. Once in Russia, with the identification removed, the boats could quickly be sold and never seen again. This kind of trade was brisk in terms of cars, but boats were a new commodity. However, with the increasing financial wealth of the Russian middle-class, they could understand why it could be a lucrative market.

The meeting took most of the morning, after which Janis took Jussi to his hotel to check in and drop his bag. The hotel was an impressive establishment, created from a renovated convent. He decided it would suit his purposes well, at least for a couple of days or more.

Shortly afterwards, Jussi rejoined Janis in the car, and they sped off towards the coastal resort of Jurmala. They parked near the seafront and found themselves on the main pedestrianised street, with a view out to sea. Jussi glanced around and approved. The air was fresh, and the place had a relaxed holiday feel to it. He was looking forward to getting to know more of Latvia during his visit, with a view to a future leisure trip.

As they walked along a small street, Janis recounted some of the town's history.

"Jurmala was the seaside retreat for important Russians in Soviet times. It was because of this that its fine old buildings were preserved. Now, due to the rising popularity of Latvia as a tourist destination, the resort has had new life breathed into it. Of course, Jurmala continues to be popular with Latvians as well."

Looking around, Jussi could tell that the architecture of the old buildings portrayed grander times, before Soviet times. He noted that the area surrounding the town was heavily wooded, and if the whole country was like this, there would be plenty of places to hide a boat.

They walked to the harbour together and spent a few minutes observing the boats and general activity. Jussi noted a few costly vessels in the area. Clearly, a few people had some serious money here.

Janis noticed him looking at the boats.

"Always, there are a few people with a lot of money. Latvia is not a wealthy country, and it is small, but still, there are some millionaires. Often their money is honestly made through hard work and innovation, but sometimes it is made in less transparent ways. Some years ago, the Russian Mafia used to control Riga. Things have improved now, but organised crime still exists and will always do so. Unfortunately, it is a part of our history and also of our future."

They bought takeaway coffees, returned to the car and turned towards the west once more. They would go to Ventspils, the industrial port of Latvia, one of the known locations of the tracking device.

On the way, Jussi quizzed Janis about police procedure in Latvia and what kind of cooperation he could expect. He gleaned that they didn't have many resources to help with international crime; however, they would try to help. Janis knew his superiors valued cooperation with Finland and emphasised this.

"How many small harbours are there in the area, Janis?" Jussi asked.

"Well, we don't have so many harbours, but we have plenty of places on the coast where someone could bring a boat ashore."

On the way, Jussi noted that the main road had many small tracks heading towards the coast through heavily wooded forests.

After a couple of hours, they arrived at the port of Ventspils and drove around the harbour. There was plenty of marine activity going on, but nothing to cause any suspicion. Following this, they visited the police station to meet with the local Chief of Police.

On arrival, they were met by a lady named Inga Kalnina; an impressive presence, who greeted the pair enthusiastically. They were shown to the lunchroom, where a meal of sausages, pancakes and paragi (bacon bread) awaited. They all tucked in and introduced themselves and their roles. Inga was keen to learn the history of the case. After questioning and listening to Jussi, she summarised her thoughts.

"Clearly, they are bringing the boats to Latvia, renewing and re-registering them in some way. Then they sell them on elsewhere, probably to Russia."

"You could be right, Inga," Jussi nodded. "How are they getting them out of Finland and into Latvia without anyone noticing, though? And without us being able to find them? We even followed one boat, and after a short while, it seemed to disappear into thin air."

"Yes, that's a mystery," she nodded. "We'll need to think about that. In the meantime, you'll have the cooperation of my highly effective police force here in Ventspils. If the boats come here, we will find them."

Jussi smiled and nodded in appreciation. At least, one of his main tasks seemed to have gone well. He had established good cooperation with the Latvian police force and with the local teams in key areas. He had also briefed those involved. Now, he needed to make some progress with the investigation itself.

Following their meeting, they visited some areas around Ventspils and then made for Riga once more. Jussi wanted to check some of the smaller places along the way, so they turned off into minor roads from time to time. These roads or tracks, as they often were, invariably led into the forest and ultimately to the coast, where one or more wooden cottages would stand. There was sometimes a boat visible but not of the type that might interest the criminals.

In the early evening, they arrived back in Riga, and Janis dropped him at his accommodation.

◆ ◆ ◆

That night, after eating in the hotel restaurant, Jussi took a walk around the old centre of Riga. He had forgotten how picturesque the city was, with its ancient buildings and colourful grand central square.

After his short excursion, he returned to the hotel, where he took a small beer in the bar and sank into a comfortable chair. His mind wandered to Heli and then to Selma in turn. He decided to make plans for Midsummer and texted Selma to ask her to join him.

Hey Selma, how about coming to Rauma with me for Midsummer?

After this trip, he decided a visit home would allow him to visit his house, do a quick check-in at the police station, and have some time and space together with Selma. He hoped that she would say yes to his suggestion. He checked online and found a small cottage on Lake Pyhjärvi, near Eura, which would be ideal.

As soon as he decided on it, a text appeared from Selma.

"Love to. Send me dates/times X."

Jussi sent the dates and booked the cottage he had just been reviewing, for a three-day break.

This will be perfect, he decided.

◆ ◆ ◆

The following day, Janis collected Jussi at 8 am from the hotel. They visited the police station first and met some other members of the Latvian force. The plan was to contact some the locally-known criminals, who owed them favours of various kinds. They would ask if they knew anything about the boat thefts or related shootings. The locals would do most of the leg work; however, there was also a meeting that Janis and Jussi would attend.

It was with one Sergey Ivanov. He was a known local 'fence' of higher value items, and there was a chance he might help them in return for the police overlooking certain issues.

They arrived at Ivanov's office at just after 10.30 am. It was located in a large, traditional but expensive-looking building on Brivibas Iela (Brivibas Street). They buzzed the office entry button, and the door opened. They took the lift up to the top floor and were met by an immaculate, attractive young woman in a silver blouse matched with black satin trousers.

She welcomed them and brought them into an open foyer with colourful armchairs and artwork. Then, she showed them into a large corner office, where she asked them to take a seat.

In contrast to the vivid entrance, this room was simply black and white. It was decorated with many photographs on the walls in black frames, apparently capturing their host, Sergey Ivanov, with various famous people, including at least one country's president.

While they were admiring the pictures, in walked their owner.

"Good Morning to you both!" he announced, with a heavy Russian accent.

"Good Morning Sergey, it's good to see you," replied Janis.

He duly introduced Jussi. Sergey made a big show of

welcoming Jussi and bade them take a seat.

"Tea, coffee, water, vodka?" he asked.

"Perhaps just coffee would suffice. Thank you," replied Jussi.

He had the feeling that vodka was often involved in Sergey's business meetings.

"So, I already know what I can do for you. Have the papers been approved?" Sergey asked Janis, at which Janis nodded and handed over an envelope.

Jussi wasn't sure what the papers were or what they related to but decided it was best to remain quiet in the circumstances. It looked as though some favour was being exchanged.

"Perfect," said Sergey, rubbing his hands together. "Now, here is what I know. Your boats are being stolen from Finland and Sweden, mainly from Helsinki and Stockholm, together with some smaller locations. It is a relatively new operation but one that is expected to make those responsible quite wealthy. One of their team recently tried to take one of the boats for himself, with some cargo it contained, actually drugs, but he was found and shot, trying to get away."

Jussi looked at Janis in some amazement as that particular piece of the puzzle clicked into place.

Sergey continued, "Next, the boats themselves are landed here in Latvia. I'm not sure where but it's somewhere close to Riga. The boats are then changed sufficiently to be resold elsewhere. They may be repainted or parts swopped with other boats, or some key elements of their specification changed. They are then moved to Russia, often in pieces, where they are reassembled and sold."

Sergey sat back with a flourish and let the two detectives absorb his news. At that moment, the receptionist walked in carrying the coffees, together with some cakes and biscuits.

"Ah, perfect timing, Inese, thank you," he said as she placed the tray on the table and then withdrew with a smile.

"I'm not going to ask you how you know this, Sergey, as you obviously have your own sources, but do you know any of the names involved?" Jussi asked politely.

"I'm sorry, I know someone who is connected in a minor way to the operation, but he will be in danger if I reveal any identities. This is all I can tell you for the moment. It is quite a lot, though, yes?"

"It certainly helps, but if you want us to continue to overlook some of your activities, we will need to know a name," said Janis.

"Hmmm, I'll see what I can do," replied Sergey. "I can't promise anything, though. This is dangerous work, you understand?"

"Okay, let's leave it for now, and I look forward to meeting again soon," ended Janis.

They shook hands and thanked Sergey, as he pressed a buzzer, and Inese appeared within seconds to show them out.

"Oh, one last thing," Sergey called out to them. "This organization who runs everything. They are called Gadyuki, or in English: the Vipers."

The two detectives looked at each other, raising their eyebrows as they walked out. When they were out of the building, Janis updated Jussi.

"It's always a fine line with this kind of person. We have enough evidence in our file to put him in prison immediately, and he knows it. However, people like him are also our best connection to the world of serious organised crime. Sergey, for example, is very well connected. In return for a few favours, he can provide information on those that would do far worse than he would ever do. By doing so, he also has the added benefit of reducing competitors from his own field of business."

Jussi nodded, realising he still had much to learn about the boundaries of law enforcement. He didn't necessarily agree with Janis but understood why this situation might be necessary. In any event, the meeting had been worthwhile.

Firstly, it had confirmed what they already knew. Secondly, it had pinpointed the landing location close to Riga, which they had suspected. Thirdly, it had provided some new information about how the boats were being sent to Russia. Finally, the Stockholm connection was entirely new to them. They hadn't been aware of any boat thefts from Sweden. The task force would now have to contact the Swedish police and bring them into the investigation. It would need to become a combined effort, now with three countries bearing down on the problem.

Unfortunately, they were still unclear on how the boats were getting to Riga across the Baltic Sea or how the parts were being transported to Russia. However, the criminal's business model was becoming more apparent, and now they knew who they were: the Vipers.

The two detectives discussed the day's findings over lunch at a small restaurant just off Riga's main square. They ate a hearty meal of local meat and potato stew with black bread. Jussi particularly enjoyed the bread and made a mental note to buy some and bring it back to Finland for midsummer.

In the early afternoon, they reconvened with the Latvian police officers they had met earlier that morning. Although their own meeting in the morning had been productive, little more helpful information had appeared from any other direction.

Janis answered Jussi's questioning expression when he asked about the criminal organisation.

"We are aware of the Vipers but have little knowledge about

them, other than knowing it is very well-connected. It is based in Saint Petersburg, and we believe the leader left the Russian Mafia to begin the group. It also seems that the Vipers are more interested in working like the gangs from the old days, by smuggling and theft, with major consequences for anyone who gets in their way. Nowadays, most older crime syndicates are more likely to be connected to real estate and international share-dealing. They frown on this kind of gang."

At the end of the meeting, Jussi summarised.

"Okay, it would be helpful if you could put together everything you know about the Vipers, together with the other information, in a file which I can take to Finland. We're going to need a name, though; before we can find out what's happening, otherwise we can only hope to get lucky. In the meantime, I will ensure some follow-up with the police in Stockholm and see if they can bring any new information to the table."

Everyone nodded and left to continue their various tasks. Jussi turned to Janis.

"I think I'll return to Helsinki on tonight's flight. It seems there is little to be gained from me staying here until we have some new information. Then, I can properly report back to the team in Finland. Thank you, Janis, this had been a valuable trip, and I have a feeling that I will be returning soon."

"And we have Jani and Ligua midsummer Celebrations this weekend and you have Juhannus too. Enjoy your weekend!" said Janis.

"You too," Jussi shook his hand, "You too!"

While he had been in Riga, Jussi had described the Juhannus event to Janis, and he had returned the compliment, comparing their celebrations of Jani and Ligua. They had agreed they were remarkably similar and involved bonfires, saunas, grilling meat and drinking beer. It seemed they were both equally looking forward to that weekend, especially as neither would be working.

◆ ◆ ◆

Later that afternoon, Jussi left for the airport and sat in the taxi, considering the next course of action. With Midsummer coming up, it was unlikely anything would be done during the following days. After briefing everyone the next day, he would write up his report and look forward to returning home to Rauma. Then, there would be a weekend in the countryside to look forward to.

Jussi's return to Helsinki was straightforward, and he arrived late in the evening at his apartment. Tomorrow he would be at work, and the next day would finish early, enabling him to meet Selma and start their time together. He had also received a message from his Uncle Hannu, who had asked him to come for dinner one evening at his own Mökki (summer cottage). It had been a while since Jussi had seen him, and he was looking forward to it. Yes, it would be good to get away for a few days.

MIDSUMMER NIGHT

The next day at the station, Jussi briefed the Task Force on his visit to Riga. They were suitably impressed about how well everything had gone. The relationship with the Latvian Police force would no doubt be a critical factor in the progress of the investigation. Also, with some new facts on the table, a clearer picture had started to form. During the meeting, Pekka had drawn the progress visually on the smartboard in the meeting room. Looking at their work, the team felt happy they had moved forward.

There had not been any more thefts in the last days, which gave them some breathing space. The harbours would be busy at this time of year, so they had drafted in extra uniformed police patrols to enable everyone, hopefully, to enjoy the midsummer Juhannus celebrations.

◆ ◆ ◆

Selma had arranged to collect Jussi from his apartment in the centre of the city and drive to Rauma. Jussi had offered to either hire a car or drive himself, but she insisted on taking the wheel. As Jussi was already learning about her strong character, he agreed.

She arrived as planned at 10 am, and Jussi was ready and waiting on the pavement, dressed in blue jeans and a green polo shirt. He also had a leather hold-all containing some essentials for the weekend, which he dropped into the boot of her convertible. They exchanged greetings as Jussi hopped into the car, and Selma set the GPS for Rauma. He noted, as usual, that she was dressed in a style that commanded attention: tight denim shorts with a white cotton shirt tied off at the waist. The sun was shining now, and it was already twenty-two degrees, an uncommonly high temperature for midsummer. Life was good.

As the day was pleasant, they took the old road towards Pori. This allowed them to avoid motorway speeds and keep the top down on Selma's car to enjoy the sun. It also meant that Selma could drive slow enough to talk on the way. Jussi noted that Selma enjoyed being the driver. She positively punched the accelerator on the quieter roads, with her hair trailing in the sunshine.

After about three hours, including a brief stop for a cold drink, they arrived in Rauma. Jussi looked around as they entered the old town. He smiled as he took in the buildings and streets that he knew so well and directed Selma to drive to his apartment. He had missed this place.

It was strange walking back into his home, especially with someone new. Everything was familiar but lacked some life. He opened some windows to let in some fresh air and brought in the bags. They would stay here this evening, and Jussi would check in with some old colleagues at the station in the morning.

They had decided on a tour of Rauma, conducted by Jussi, followed by a supermarket visit to stock up on provisions. Then, it would be time to go onwards to their chosen cottage. However, now, it was time to eat.

After a brief stop at Jussi's house, they strolled down Kuninkaankatu, the main pedestrianized street of the old town. Jussi wasn't sure how it happened, but they walked hand in hand down the old cobbled street. He stopped on the square for a moment and looked at the museum. He remembered the event that had started the case of 'The Paintings of Rauma' and shook his head with some disbelief, smiling to himself.

They walked further down the street and arrived at a small restaurant. It had recently opened and appeared to be quite popular. They managed to find a table for two, and Jussi related his story about the case once more. Selma seemed even more fascinated, and he felt justified in explaining more than he had done previously. He thought she probably had no idea about what police work involved, so he explained how the case had required much commitment and many hours of research. He was pleasantly surprised at how easily Selma seemed to accept this, which was necessary for anyone involved with a detective.

"And? In the end, did you ever hear from Heli?" asked Selma after the story had finished.

"No, nothing has been heard from her since," he lied convincingly.

He justified this to himself that it would serve no purpose to tell her otherwise, even though he was still occasionally in telephone contact. Also, he didn't want to admit that he still had feelings for her.

They finished eating and wandered back along the street. It was quiet. Perhaps many of the residents had already left for their Midsummer break. The couple returned to Jussi's apartment, and he was reminded of how much he had enjoyed their first night together.

◆ ◆ ◆

Jussi awoke the following day and dressed, leaving a note for Selma as she continued to sleep.

Gone to the station. See you later. Enjoy your morning, Jussi.

He left the note on the table where she would see it. He then drank his coffee and took the familiar walk to the Rauma Police

Station.

Jussi was happy to see his old colleagues, Pekka, Tuomas, and especially Harri, at the station. He also met Maarit, who had been his superior in Rauma. She was very complimentary about what she had heard about his career progress.

"Well, we are honoured that Jussi Alonen, the great detective from Helsinki, has come to see us," announced Harri, pulling Jussi's leg.

Jussi felt immediately comfortable and found himself wondering if he would want to return here one day.

After a couple of hours catch-up, together with a plentiful supply of coffee and pulla buns, he reluctantly bade the team farewell and left for his apartment.

When he arrived home, he found Selma sitting on the sofa, reading with her E-reader.

"Well, hey there, how was your reunion?" she asked.

"It was great, thanks, just great. It's amazing how you can leave somewhere for a few months and walk back in feeling as if you just left yesterday."

They repacked, jumped in the car and drove to the supermarket to collect some essentials, including a visit to Alko, the state-owned alcoholic drinks store. They bought some meats to grill, salad ingredients and some bottles of wine, beer and cider, the latter being Selma's favourite. Then, it was off to the cottage.

◆ ◆ ◆

After about forty minutes, they arrived. Jussi was happy with his choice of cottage. The mökki was situated right by the lake. It had a new pier that extended far into the water, directly from the sauna. It was an old cottage built with heavy logs, and inside it had a large fireplace in the living room; everything was very cosy.

"This is perfect," Selma said with a smile and gave him a peck on the cheek.

"Not too shabby." remarked Jussi. "But wait until you see my uncle's place! Let's unpack and get changed. He's expecting us soon, and we shouldn't be late; he might already be grilling some nice steaks."

"Do we drive there?" Selma asked.

"Nope. We go on bikes," Jussi gestured to the adjoining building. "It's only a couple of kilometres to his place, and we'll be there in fifteen minutes. It also means we can both have a few glasses of something while we're there."

"Now you're talking," she said, with a cheeky grin on her face.

After dropping their gear, Selma changed clothes. She came out of the bedroom wearing a simple white shirt dress, with a blue belt and her hair tied back with a blue ribbon. Jussi nodded, approving of her attire, and they left with the bikes from the storage shed. The bicycles were old and rattled all the way, but they managed with them, with the help of a few laughs.

A little later, they arrived at a large timber cottage with several out-buildings. The main cabin had a commanding view of the lake from its elevated position. Jussi remembered seeing this place many times when he was younger. There had been a time when he had spent many weekends here as a child. However, his parents and uncle seemed to drift apart for some reason, and his visits became more infrequent as he grew older. Now, he remembered he hadn't been here for at least ten years.

As they arrived at the terrace, his uncle was already grilling meat on an enormous barbeque. Uncle Hannu looked just as

Jussi had remembered him. He was wearing a black chef's apron with a glass of red wine in one hand and grilling tongs in the other. The barbeque was spitting oil and smoke as he turned over the steaks.

"Jussi!" he exclaimed as the couple stepped onto the deck.

He put down the glass and tongs and greeted Jussi warmly while making a big show of how pretty Selma was, making her blush profusely.

"Uncle Hannu, you haven't changed a bit," Jussi exclaimed.

"Well, maybe a little greyer here and there," he replied with a grin.

"What a beautiful place," said Selma, looking around at the cottage and the lake.

"Thank you," he replied, smiling. "It's been a lifetime's work; you might say."

He bade them sit at the long heavy table on the terrace, pouring generous glasses of red wine for each. Jussi looked around and noted that they were the only guests for the evening, judging by the place settings. On the grill were some large steaks, sweetcorn and halloumi cheese. There was also a large salad on the table with some fresh bread. The aroma was delicious.

"You're just in time," his Uncle said, removing the steaks from the grill.

The three of them tucked into delicious rib-eye steaks and fresh salad, washed down with, first one and then a second bottle of Amarone red wine. They chatted about various topics of life in Helsinki and Jussi and Selma's jobs.

The subject of the 'Paintings of Rauma' arose, and they discussed this for some time. Selma smiled and shook her head in disbelief at the story, despite hearing it again. Jussi apologised to her and was concerned that she might have become bored by it, but she still seemed to hang on to his every word.

"Well, who would have thought that a boy from Rauma would end up as an international detective," Uncle Hannu smiled.

"From Eura," Jussi corrected him.

"From Rauma," Uncle Hannu firmly reminded him. Jussi looked puzzled. He continued, "When you were very young, your father had to move to Eura to take over the family business. You were actually born in Rauma, but you spent your life in Eura. Now you've returned home."

"Well, why didn't anyone tell me this?" Jussi questioned.

"Your Father's business suffered a terrible loss when a company illegally withdrew from a contract. He tried his best to recover but unfortunately went bankrupt. Your grandfather helped your family to move to Eura to begin again. We didn't talk about those times much after that."

"So, I'm a Raumalainen (from Rauma), Jussi laughed. "Not that it's so important, as Eura has always been good to me. I feel as if I've got two homes now. I wondered why I was such a big Lukko (Rauma Ice Hockey Team) fan!"

They all laughed, and the glasses were refilled. They talked some more, and when Selma retired to the bathroom, Uncle Hannu leaned over to Jussi.

"You've struck gold there, young man. Don't lose this one!" He continued, "You know, I've been thinking, I have nobody to leave this place to. Would you like it, Jussi?"

"What! I hope you aren't going anywhere for a while, Uncle Hannu!" Jussi replied, taken aback.

"No, not yet, but it would mean a lot to me if I could leave you this place. It should be in safe hands and stay in the family. I don't want it to end up with a stranger," he said, offering his hand to be shaken.

Jussi reciprocated the handshake with gratitude. He was happy that he had re-established communications with his uncle, more than anything else.

Selma returned at that moment, and they decided it was getting late. After a fine dinner and several glasses of wine, they should make tracks for their cottage whilst they still could. They thanked Uncle Hannu for his hospitality, took their bikes and slowly made their way back along the forest track.

They were both tired when they arrived at the cabin, and any passion had evaporated on the journey. They quickly prepared for bed, and Selma fell asleep almost immediately. Jussi lay pondering the evening's discussions for a few minutes before his eyes closed, having decided that he should definitely spend more time with his uncle in future. Time had gone fast, and Jussi hadn't realized. As he had been growing older, so his uncle had too. He resolved to return to Rauma, and Eura, every couple of months from now on. It had been good to see his favourite places once more. With that thought, he fell sound asleep.

❖ ❖ ❖

The next morning, Jussi and Selma awoke late and agreed it had been a fine evening.

After a leisurely breakfast, they decided to have a morning sauna. First, they went outside to make a vihta (a birch whip). They would use this (as is traditional in Finland) to lightly whip each other while in the heat of the sauna.

Their day proceeded with several swimming sessions, moving between the sauna and the lake. They agreed that beer and sausages would be perfect for lunch. Their Finnish midsummer together was well underway.

◆ ◆ ◆

After an enjoyable morning, they set up the grill and prepared lunch. Even though the barbeque was small and took some time to get going, Jussi was determined to grill his selection of meats outside. Selma prepared potatoes and a salad in the kitchen inside and arranged the table.

True to form, as many a Finnish midsummer could testify, a drizzle of rain began to fall, and it took a while to complete the cooking. Jussi was happy enough, though, as he stood over his gourmet feast with a beer.

When he had finished, Selma was waiting and already midway through her third glass of wine when Jussi made his grand entrance and laid the food on the table. They clinked their drinks together in a midsummer's toast.

Some of Jussi's old friends were staying at another cottage across the lake and had invited them to join. However, they decided to meet them for dinner instead, because after several glasses of wine, they felt unable to cycle the distance. So, they curled up on the sofa together and found other entertainment.

◆ ◆ ◆

The following morning passed quickly. Jussi and Selma slept in again and decided to drive over for lunch with Jussi's friends before returning to Helsinki that evening.

They enjoyed another grilled feast. Jussi talked of nothing in particular but had a great time, and the gang were impressed with Selma.

"It's about time someone snagged this guy," one of his friends joked, at which the couple laughed with some embarrassment.

By 5 pm, they were on the road again and driving back to Helsinki. It took three hours, which they drove direct. The plan was to spend the night at Selma's apartment and enjoy a quiet night in. The weekend had been a good one, and they were both quite tired.

They arrived, unpacked, opened some of the remaining snacks with a bottle of wine and settled down to watch a movie. Jussi found himself wondering why he hadn't thought of Heli over the whole weekend until now, that is. It seemed that Selma was good for him in more ways than he had initially thought. He glanced over and smiled at her face, now leaning on his shoulder, fast asleep.

LUCKY BREAK

Jussi and Selma said their goodbyes on the following day, as both had separate plans for their final day off. She was meeting an old girlfriend, and he had some things to organise. Jussi had been vague about his plans, as he didn't want to become too attached, at least not just yet. He liked his space and was happy she would be busy that day.

He spent the afternoon on his laptop, going over some details of the case. There had been a few updates in the file but nothing special. He did note something of interest, though, not about boats but bicycles instead. It seemed that someone had been reported by the public, having been noticed moving bikes between bushes. The suspects had subsequently been arrested and were now in custody - charged with theft. Jussi was interested to read this and planned to talk to the suspect the following morning. At least this was one win for the team, who were currently under some pressure.

That evening, Jussi cooked a simple meal of rice and beans, and spent time in his apartment, catching up with some chores. He was strangely missing Selma, but turned his attention to his laptop instead.

◆ ◆ ◆

The next morning, Jussi made his way to the police station and spent time catching up with colleagues in the small kitchen. The initial conversations centred around everyone's midsummer activities. It seemed that all had an enjoyable break, and there was much to discuss about that.

When the subject finally turned towards work, the two issues at hand were, unsurprisingly, boats and bikes. It was a relief for all to discover there had been no more stolen vessels. As they had wondered, the criminals had also taken the weekend off. Tapio also suggested that the gang may have decided to take a break, if they had felt the police getting closer. The others nodded in agreement.

"How about our bicycle thieves?" Jussi asked.

Jonas, one of the team, replied, "Well, we have one of them downstairs now, and he'll probably admit it. He couldn't really do anything else. He was carrying a bike at the time, from one bush to another, with more bikes stashed behind them. We're hoping to extract the names of the others involved in exchange for offering a lighter sentence."

"That's great," Jussi said. "Could I talk to him as well, just to wrap a few things up and update the file?"

"Don't see why not," he replied. "Just make sure you arrange to talk to him with the arresting officer, so we have all our ducks in a row."

Jussi nodded and drained his coffee. He then took a trip down to the main uniformed division office in order to locate the arresting officer of the bicycle thief. Within a few minutes, he had found the officer in question, who was Stefan Hämäläinen. Together, they discussed the case.

Stefan was a smart young officer, clearly ambitious, who appreciated the opportunity of working with a detective on the case. Usually, this would be all that would be required in this situation, and Jussi would turn his file over to Stefan. However, Jussi was quite keen to pursue the rest of the gang, and Stefan agreed that it would be of value for them both to be present at the following interview. Stefan would make the arrangements, and as the detainee had already contracted a lawyer, an interview would be arranged with all parties. Stefan thought he could set it quickly and promised it would happen either in the afternoon or the next day.

Surprisingly, no sooner had Jussi got settled at his desk than Stefan called back and advised that the interview would be at 2 pm that afternoon. Jussi thanked him, entered it in his diary and returned his attention to boats. His thoughts returned to Latvia, and he opened the large-scale map on the meeting table once again. He surveyed the known routes between Helsinki and Riga and from Riga to Saint Petersburg. Although the channel didn't look very wide on the map, it was a vast expanse of water, and he wondered how they would be able to determine the exact route. It seemed they would have to rely on finding a potential suspect through conversations within the Finnish and Latvian underworld, or just be plain lucky and catch them in the act. He updated the file accordingly. As it was already lunchtime, he decided to take lunch in the canteen before the bicycle thief interview.

◆ ◆ ◆

After lunch: a tasty steak with chips, Jussi made his way to the lower floor, where the cells and interview rooms were housed. He met Stefan, and together they made their way to Interview Room 3, where the prisoner was being held.

Ari Mäkinen was a career criminal. At the age of 15, he was arrested for car theft, and things had gone rapidly downhill from there. Now 26, he had already been in prison for five years of his life. He was heavily tattooed and wore a smug expression wherever he went as if he knew something everyone else didn't. He sat slumped in a chair, tapping on the table, when Jussi and Stefan entered the room.

"Moro," (Hello) Ari greeted them, the sides of his mouth curling upwards as he did so.

Jussi instantly disliked the man but professional as he was, sat at the table and smiled back at him.

"So, what is this? Have you have brought some reinforcements?" he asked Stefan.

Stefan smiled and introduced Jussi as the Detective who had been leading the investigation. Ari's lawyer, who had until now been sitting quietly in the corner of the room, introduced herself as Mirka Mononen. She was smartly dressed and wore a black suit, together with a highly professional demeanour. They shook hands, and Ari regarded Jussi with some interest. Then he asked something Jussi did not expect.

"So, are you the one who is interested in stolen boats?" Ari asked.

Jussi's eyes opened wider and he moved a little closer to the table.

"What do you know about stolen boats?" he asked, somewhat dismissively.

"More than you, maybe?" Ari answered with a sneer.

"If you know anything about that, now is the time to talk. If you tell me something interesting, we can tell the Judge you've been cooperating with the police. They might be more lenient on you," said Jussi.

"I think that what I know is worth a little more than that," Ari replied. Then continued, "And if I did tell you, you would have to take me far, far away, so they couldn't get to me."

"Who couldn't get to you?" asked Stefan, now also more interested.

"The boys in black, from Saint Petersburg," he answered. "If I tell you what I know, I'll be dead before the week is out. You'll have to offer me something much more."

His lawyer interrupted with a warning to Ari that he was being recorded and he was not under any obligation to reveal any additional information.

"It's okay," Ari said. "I know what I'm doing. I think I hold the winning cards."

"Really? What can you tell me then?" Jussi asked impatiently.

"Hmmm. What if I told you that I knew who was taking the boats and where they were taking them."

At this, Ari sat back with an air of some superiority.

"If you tell us that. Perhaps, we may be able to do something with your sentence," Jussi replied.

"You're not listening to me, are you? Have you heard of the Russian Mafia, Jussi? Did you think that they all became white-collar investors? Let me tell you, there are still some left, and this particular gang is more than nasty. I have no wish to end up dead in my bed one morning. They would find me, whether I would be in prison or on the run. If I give you this information, I need you to guarantee that you'll get me as far away as possible and drop all of the charges for the bikes."

"Come on, Ari; we're hardly going to put you in a witness protection program over some stolen bikes, or even boats," Stefan remarked with disdain.

"You think it's a few stolen boats?" Ari replied. "Firstly, they've been doing this for some months already; they have just been subtle about it. Now, they know they can get away with it; the orders are increasing. Also, they've done this in several places and other countries. After this, they intend to progress to trade stolen cars, drugs and women."

He waited for a moment, for effect.

"Oh and, expensive stolen bikes too. Their business empire includes lots of things and is worth millions."

Jussi paused the conversation and nodded to Stefan to go outside. They discussed the situation and Jussi called Tapio downstairs to join them in the adjoining room. They could see Ari squirming in his seat, looking directly at the two-way mirror. His lawyer had reminded Ari again that there was no need to talk further. Still, he had dismissed the advice in preference of his own.

They re-entered the interview room, with Tapio in the adjacent office, already on the phone to the Detective Inspector. Jussi sat down, and passed a coffee to Ari, which was gratefully received.

"Right, interview re-commenced at 3 pm. Ari, do you admit to the bicycle thefts and are you willing to inform us of your fellow criminals in this matter?" asked Jussi.

"No, I bloody won't. I won't rat out my friends. Now that you've caught me, they'll stop for a while anyway, so why don't we talk about the more interesting matter?"

Ari stamped the table with his fist as he pronounced the final word, spilling some of the coffee as he did so.

"Why don't we just relax?" Stefan asked politely.

Mirka leaned over and touched Ari's shoulder. He nodded his head in agreement.

"Okay, okay," he said. "This is my offer. You will drop all the charges against me and give me a new identity together with enough money to get far away from here. You need to understand that this all leads to some powerful and wealthy people. People who want to expand their criminal organization into Finland. Is that what you want? I can help you to stop it."

They took another short break to talk strategy, but it was evident that Ari wasn't going to tell them anything without knowing exactly what he would get in return.

The team decided to call it a day and let Ari stew in the cell for another night. They thanked the lawyer, arranged for another interview the next day and left the room. Now, they needed approval from higher up. The opportunity of catching serious criminals far outweighed this little fish, but they didn't know whether their superiors would agree to make a deal to get the information they desired.

They bid each other goodnight, and Jussi left for home. Just before he left the station, he noted he had received another call from Heli. He was beginning to get frustrated with these calls, especially from someone who would remain out of reach no matter how he felt about her.

He scrolled down his phone and saw a message from Selma. It was a cartoon of a woman blowing a kiss. Jussi laughed and made his decision there and then. He pressed the button to block Heli's phone number and returned Selma's message with an equally amusing picture. After that, he smiled and left the building.

NARROW ESCAPE

Jussi felt like being alone, as he sometimes did. He had friends, and now he had Selma, but equally, he liked to have space to arrange his own activities. This evening, he felt like some fresh air, so after returning to his apartment to change, he made his way to the kayak centre.

He breathed a sigh of satisfaction as he pushed off the beach into the waves. He paddled for some time but failed to detach from his thoughts about either work or women. However, he enjoyed the space and freedom from being out on the water. With the evening remaining light, he would be able to stay out here for a couple of hours or more.

As he continued, he recognised the island where he and Selma had eaten their picnic and paddled towards it. As he did so, he became aware of the sound of a powerful engine approaching.

"That's going to cause some waves," Jussi complained under his breath. He has the whole sea around him, and he has to come that close to me."

Jussi began to speed up, his paddle mechanically dipping in and out of the water as he powered through the swell towards land.

Suddenly, the boat veered towards him and rapidly closed in. Jussi cursed and continued to paddle, this time without thinking, as fast as he could do so. As he was moving, he calculated that he wouldn't get there in time.

The motor launch suddenly lurched forward and headed directly towards Jussi's kayak at a 45-degree angle. He called out but couldn't make out anyone in the boat. Within a few seconds, he felt it crash into his craft, breaking it into pieces and rolling it over.

Mentally and physically, he had already tensed himself and was prepared to swim. Hence, as the kayak rolled over, he held his breath and pushed away from it. He swam downwards and away, into the cold sea, until he had to surface for air.

There was nothing to be seen when he did - except for a few remains of broken yellow kayak fragments floating in the water, about twenty metres from where he was. He turned around, pointed himself towards shore and began to swim.

The sound of an engine came into earshot once more, and he saw a boat coming towards him again. He was just preparing to dive when it slowed down. Then, he saw a hand waving over the side and heard a girl shouting.

"Come here, come aboard," she called.

Jussi swam to the boat and was helped onboard by the girl and a tall, smiling man.

"Are you okay?" she asked.

"We saw the whole thing," the man said, in an English accent.

The girl continued, "I can't believe it. It drove straight at you, and then after it had smashed into your boat, it turned around and left you for dead."

Jussi collapsed on the rear seat of the boat, shivering. The girl, introducing herself as Petra, placed a warm coat over his shoulders. The Englishman introduced himself as John and offered him a coffee, which was gratefully received. It was a hot, strong brew, and he clasped it with both hands as they headed across the sea to the harbour and safety.

◆ ◆ ◆

When Jussi arrived at his apartment that night, he was still shocked that someone had deliberately rammed him.

Could it be somehow connected with the boats or the witness, Ari? he thought. *What other possible reason would anyone have to try and kill him? Also, he was a police officer, so the people who did this must be getting desperate.*

He had already taken a shower at the harbour visitors' facilities and borrowed some dry clothes. Next, he made calls to the kayak centre, the coast guard and the police station. He had declined medical attention at the time, as remarkably, he had escaped without a scratch. However, Tapio told him he should take some time off to get properly checked by a doctor.

After making the calls, Jussi decided he would file the paperwork later on. Right now, he needed to sleep in a warm bed.

◆ ◆ ◆

Jussi awoke in the morning with a thumping headache. He went to the bathroom and checked his head in the mirror. No, he hadn't banged it anywhere, and there was no sign of a bruise or blood. He took an aspirin and returned to bed. Checking his watch, it was almost 9 am. He switched on the coffee maker and took a shower.

After his shower and a double expresso, Jussi felt a little better. He sat down and relaxed on the sofa with his laptop, checking his e-mails and surfing the online news. He was relieved to find that the incident hadn't made the news as nothing had been reported.

Following Tapio's orders, he got ready to visit the local medical centre for a check-up. After that, he would write up his statement and try and relax for a while. He would also call Selma but not until later when he had fully recovered. He still felt shaken; it wasn't every day that someone attempted to kill you.

◆ ◆ ◆

Hemmo and Samuli were sitting outside a café, by the sea, close to the upmarket area of Helsinki named Eira. They were seated at a simple plastic table, drinking coffee and snacking on pulla buns.

"Well, if that doesn't stop him, nothing will," Samuli remarked.

Hemmo replied, "At least it should keep him off the trail for a while. He was getting too close and too interested. We need to keep the boats moving, or someone is going to become unhappy, and our payday will come to an end."

"Is it possible we can continue with this number of boats? Two every week is a lot," commented Samuli.

"I'm not sure," replied Hemmo, drumming his fingers on the table. "Maybe for the meantime, if we keep moving around. Later on, it will mean taking a few more risks. The risks may begin to outweigh the rewards at some stage, though. Perhaps after the next couple, we should visit Mariehamn, as we discussed? Stockholm was such a long-haul last time."

"I like that idea. It's a quiet place, plenty of boats, less security and still not too far from Riga," agreed Samuli.

"I'll talk to Edgars, "Another coffee?"

◆ ◆ ◆

Edgars looked out to sea. He was hoping for another boat within the next two days. The demand from Saint Petersburg was becoming incessant, and although he was on target, they still demanded more. On the positive side, his cash reserves were increasing nicely. He couldn't wait to get to the point when he had enough money to do other things; less risky ones where he didn't need to be so closely involved. Gregor had insisted that he didn't divert any of his revenue from Latvia as the Finnish project should be successful in its own right. This business was a start-up in every way and had to be self-funded.

"I suppose that's how Gregor makes so much money," he remarked into thin air as the sea breeze blew gently into his face.

The telephone rang. It was Hemmo.

"Hemmo, how's it going?"

"All good here, Edgars. Although, I think we need a change of plan," Hemmo replied.

Edgars waited for a few moments for him to continue.

"We took out the detective who has been following our tracks, and hopefully, it will buy us some more time."

"Good," said Edgars, "So I'll be receiving another boat soon?"

"Well, soon enough, but I want to move our operations to Mariehamn. Helsinki is getting too hot, and it'll give us space to continue with less risk."

"Less risk for you, you mean?" Edgars responded. "We have further to travel there and back, and it's much slower at night, negotiating all of those islands. I remember Stockholm - that was painful."

"Yes, but if we're caught? Then that's it, isn't it?"

"Perhaps I should find myself some guys who have the guts to continue when things get a bit difficult? I think I'm paying you enough," Edgars remarked.

"Mariehamn is further for us to travel also, you know. What if we accept a slightly lower fee?"

At this, Samuli shot him a disapproving look. Hemmo shook his head.

"Alright, I suppose it would be a better option for the moment, and if you offset my fuel and time costs, then I can agree. Let's say 7000€ per boat from Mariehamn then?"

Hemmo took a sharp intake of breath and considered this for a moment.

"Alright, that's fine; Does it goes back up again when we return to Helsinki?"

"Yes, we can agree that. I just can't have any interruption in supply. The boats need to keep coming; you understand, Hemmo?" Edgars spoke slowly and deliberately to emphasise the point.

Hemmo agreed and rang off.

Following the phone conversation, there was a short but heated discussion between Hemmo and Samuli about the lower fee; however, Samuli accepted that there had been no choice. They both knew it was better not to fall foul of Edgars or anyone else in the chain of command of that particular organisation.

◆ ◆ ◆

At the Medical Centre, Jussi had received a clean bill of health. After picking up a few things from the local supermarket, he returned home. He still felt tired but was keen to return to the matter of interviewing the bike thief. When Jussi had not returned to the station after the kayaking incident, the thief had refused to talk to anyone else. He had apparently developed some level of trust, and Jussi was keen not to let this relationship get cold. Anyway, for the moment, he was under orders to rest.

He decided to call Selma; no doubt she would brighten his day.

"Hi, Jussi," Selma answered.

"Hi Selma, how are you?" Jussi greeted her.

"All good. What's up?"

Jussi explained about the incident and how he was resting at his place. She was shocked and asked how he was, and was relieved to learn he had been checked by a doctor and was alright.

"Okay, I'm coming after I finish work and will fix you something to eat."

Selma didn't ask; it was a statement.

"Sounds great. Thanks, Selma. It will be great to see you."

❖ ❖ ❖

Hemmo and Samuli boarded the ferry to Mariehamn. They had booked tickets on the large overnight ferry to take them to the island of Åland.

The two criminals had booked a twin cabin and, after receiving their keys, dropped their small bags and went straight to the bar. The ferry was more like a small cruise ship and hosted several restaurants, bars and shops, hosting a mix of Finns and Swedes.

They had booked a hotel in Mariehamn for two nights, and a hire car to explore suitable targets. They planned to complete their reconnaissance mission, then steal a boat for the return trip. After this, they would return every few days, using different ferries, taking a boat on each visit. This routine would continue for a month, after which they would return to business in mainland Finland.

In the bar, they clinked glasses. They had ordered large, cold beers and planned to drink several that evening. They felt like they were on vacation now and would make the most of it.

Hemmo read from a travel brochure on the table.

"Åland is an autonomous Finnish territory lying between Finland and Sweden, within an archipelago of twenty thousand islands. Its capital and port, Mariehamn, welcomes passengers that travel between Turku in Finland and Stockholm in Sweden, docking en-route. Ferries bring tourism, commerce and supplies to the small, picturesque town."

Hemmo and Samuli both smiled, knowing their visit would probably not be so welcome.

After their drinks, they planned to dine at the fish restaurant and then bag themselves a table at the onboard nightclub. It would be a long night.

◆ ◆ ◆

Selma arrived at Jussi's apartment with a bag of groceries in hand. She had visited the delicatessen at the department store and bought prawns, salad ingredients, fresh bread, strawberries, and ice cream.

Jussi was delighted to see her, especially as she immediately set about preparing dinner, insisting that he relax. He was also happy that they seemed to be more comfortable than ever in each other's company.

It was a warm day, and Selma was wearing a pale pink fitted polo shirt and a short tan skirt with silver jewellery. He wondered if she had changed before she came or if she always looked this good at work. He was just wondering this when Selma caught him looking at her.

"Something you like?" she asked with a smile.

"Everything," Jussi replied. "I feel better already."

"I bet you do," Selma replied. "Well, you just relax for a while, okay? I'm going to spoil you tonight. You deserve it after what you have been through."

Jussi was feeling fine now but happy to agree to Selma's instructions.

Within half an hour, he was tucking into a fine meal. They had already spoken about the incident in detail, so they talked of other things such as Selma's day and possible plans.

"This case will take a while, but after that, what about going for a trip somewhere? I mean somewhere nice - a holiday. I haven't been abroad anywhere warm for a long time, and the thought really appeals to me," Jussi said.

"Well, I never need an excuse for a vacation somewhere warm," Selma replied. "Let's think about some places to go over the next few days, and we can check the internet together. I've always wanted to go to Cuba, for example."

Jussi smiled but quickly changed the subject. The mention of Cuba brought memories that he preferred not to remember. Because of Heli, the chances of Jussi going to Cuba were zero, and he even thought Selma might be testing him.

After dinner, although Jussi would have been happy for her to stay that night, Selma had to return to her apartment. She had arrived straight from work and would need to leave early again for work in the morning.

Jussi went to bed soon after she left. Tomorrow, it would be

JOHN SWALLOW

back to work, hopefully with a clearer head.

THE SNITCH

Jussi awoke early and quickly showered, dressed and grabbed a cereal bar for breakfast on his way out. He was in a hurry, so he decided to collect a coffee-to-go and drink it on the way. It was unlike Jussi to go without his customary homemade expresso in the mornings, but today, he was on a mission.

On arrival at the station, he immediately went to see the Inspector. Pekka was sitting in his corner office with an enormous mug of coffee in front of him. He was reading documents on his laptop when Jussi knocked.

"Come in, Jussi. How are you? We've all been worried about you. No ill effects, I hope, from that terrible experience?"

"I'm fine, thank you," Jussi replied. "I have a slight headache, and a strong wish to find whoever hit me, but that aside, I'm okay."

Pekka asked Jussi to tell the story once more and made a few notes as he did so. Jussi recounted the incident in as much detail as he could remember. At the end, Pekka gave his own opinion.

"I agree with you. The circumstances do suggest that this was a premeditated attack. Someone must have been following you. It can't have been a coincidence that they just happened to see you in a kayak unless they were tipped off. The incident is incredible. The penalties for attacking a police officer are high enough, and this could be classed as attempted murder!"

"Yes, it certainly felt like it from my end," Jussi answered, grimacing as he did so.

Pekka asked him to complete the file with a detailed statement. Jussi had already done some of the work at home the day before, so suggested he complete it first, and then meet the bike thief. Pekka agreed and was keen to know any helpful information the suspect may possess. They had to find a name that would bring them closer to the perpetrators. Pekka confirmed that they would be willing to consider a reduced charge if any information resulted in arrests, especially of the boat's helmsman that had hit Jussi's kayak.

Jussi had arranged to meet Stefan and assist him in the interview again. It was standard practice to have a second interviewer for these situations, and he'd been quite happy with Stefan's performance. Jussi wanted to be as involved as possible in every stage of this investigation, because now, things had become personal. In addition, the suspect, Ari, had been keen to talk to Jussi again and had instructed Stefan that he would not need a lawyer for the meeting. There were things to be said that might be necessary to keep off the record.

Stefan opened the interview with the usual formalities for the audio recording, while Jussi reviewed some new additions to the file.

"Ari, nice to see you once again. For the recording, Ari has declined that his lawyer be present at this interview, and Detective Jussi Alonen accompanies me."

Jussi moved in, "Ari, during our last interview, you offered to provide us with crucial information concerning the theft of boats from Helsinki and other locations. Is this still the case?"

Ari nodded enthusiastically, with a smile on his face.

"You should also be aware that we believe the thefts, over time, total eighteen boats, from various countries, with a total value exceeding one million euros. In addition, we believe an attempted murder of a police officer may be connected to these crimes. Namely me. Yesterday."

Jussi stared him squarely in the face. Ari was taken aback for a moment and fell silent.

"I want answers, now," demanded Jussi.

"Well, of course, I would like to help. That's terrible. I mean, I can believe they would try and kill you because of the type of people they are. If I said anything, they would do the same to me. They would probably succeed as well, using a good old-fashioned bullet." Ari replied.

"What do you want?" asked Jussi, now with more than a hint of menace in his voice.

"I want to leave Finland with a new identity and enough money to be comfortable. Otherwise, what am I going to do? If you want me to be your snitch, I can do that, but they will get to me if I stay here. These people are serious and their bosses even more so."

Jussi regarded him for a moment. Then he made the offer.

"We are prepared to reduce the charges against you in return for this information. We can also relocate you to a safe prison for a lesser term. However, we need the name today."

Ari suddenly thumped the desk.

"Hey," Stefan shouted. "That's enough. Now, calm down."

Jussi asked again, "What's it going to be, Ari?"

"You need to do better than that," he replied, shaking his head.

"Then, you need to tell me more than you're telling me," Jussi demanded.

"Alright. I'll tell you something, but the name waits until you have agreed to a deal that protects me properly."

"And....?" Jussi waited.

Ari blurted it out, "There's a gang in Helsinki that has been involved in thefts for a long time, sometimes involving boats. Now, though, things are different. It has grown into a big business, and millions of euros are involved. A Russian organisation is chasing money, and they plan to bring their criminal activities to Helsinki. Now, that's all I'm saying, except that these people are dangerous and you need to be careful. Once they decide you need to be eliminated, then that is what will happen."

Jussi and Stefan looked at each other, stopped the recording and left the room.

"Okay, this is going above my pay grade now," Jussi said. "I need to go upstairs if we have to start offering bigger deals."

Jussi left and took the elevator upwards, making a beeline for Pekka's office, once again. Pekka was on his mobile phone and beckoned him into the office as he finished the call.

"Jussi?" he asked expectantly.

"I have a request," Jussi asked.

They sat down and discussed the conversation with Ari, during which Pekka made a call to his superior. Jussi heard his name mentioned a few times. It seemed that he was getting more well-known, although he wasn't sure if it was for the right reasons. Then, Pekka gestured for him to leave the room. Jussi returned to his desk and waited, checking a few emails as he did so.

"Jussi!" Pekka called out a few minutes later.

He duly returned to the office and sat down in anticipation.

"Right. Suppose you can extract enough information,

including names, which will lead us to the boat thieves' arrest and prove the links to Russia. In that case, we will agree to his request. We can put this offer in writing before his lawyer; however, we retain the right to withdraw it if the information doesn't lead to the gang's arrest inside Finland," explained Pekka.

"So, could we get him on witness protection?" asked Jussi.

"Yes, we could. If your informer is lying, though, we'll bang him away for the rest of his miserable life as an accessory to a lot more than stealing a few bikes."

Jussi nodded. There was some considerable trust being placed in him now. He had half-expected the Inspector to either say no or to bring in a more senior detective, but he was being allowed to ride with it. He couldn't risk screwing this one up.

He returned to the interview room and the hapless Ari, where he explained the deal. Ari seemed very relieved but wanted to wait for his lawyer. A call was made to Mirka, who was available and would come to the station within the hour. Now, it was time to take a break.

After imbibing some coffee, Jussi and Stefan returned to the interview room at the appointed time, sufficiently refuelled with caffeine. In the room sat Ari and Mirka, waiting patiently for their arrival.

Jussi began, "Alright, let's get back to our discussion. I have the authority to offer you protection under the witness protection program in return for the provision of certain information. Provided your information leads to the arrest of the perpetrators of the boat thefts, murder, attempted murder and criminal damage charges. If this is the case, the bicycle theft charges against you will be suspended. However, they won't be dropped and will be reconsidered later if there is any misinformation provided or if you choose to re-offend in any way."

Ari digested this for a moment and agreed.

"Okay, so do I get to go to a beach somewhere?"

"Maybe in the north of the country, in Oulu," Jussi replied. "We're not setting you up in a life of luxury - you're a criminal, Ari. However, we can help you make a new life instead of prison for the next few years. That's as much as we are prepared to offer, do you understand?"

Ari nodded and asked to confer with his lawyer.

It was a short conversation, with the only request being to put it in writing. Jussi provided this, signed by the Detective Inspector.

"Now," Jussi said. "Tell me everything you know, including names."

Ari spent some time talking, and every so often, they questioned him further about his knowledge of the crimes. His knowledge was limited but what he did know seemed to stack up.

The story began when Ari had been scoping out potential bikes to steal. He had spent a lot of time around the places used by commuters and office workers, used to store their bikes. He had mainly looked for remote areas with few people around.

One day, he found a suitable bicycle storage area near the docks. The rack was used by office workers who worked within new offices nearby. Some of the bikes were expensive, and some even left their electric bikes there. Ari resolved to spend some time observing the place, as there could be several bikes he could remove at the same time. There was a possibility of earning thousands in one day.

On one occasion, in the evening, he happened to walk to the

local kiosk to buy cigarettes when he saw someone he knew from prison walking towards the harbour area. He met another man, and somehow, Ari knew they were up to something, so decided to follow them. He wandered slowly behind and stopped to light another cigarette. A few moments later, the two men boarded a boat and hotwired the ignition.

Within a few minutes, they were speeding out to sea. Clearly, they had stolen the vessel, and Ari was surprised they did it in broad daylight. A bike was one thing but a boat?

He watched them speed out to sea and disappear. He remembered the man from prison, although he couldn't quite recall the name. He had been a nasty character and one to keep a safe distance away from.

That evening, he met one of his friends, a Latvian ex-con, at a local bar. Ari had mentioned some boats that had been stolen recently. His friend warned him not to dig into it, as the people involved were bad news. He said he had done some jobs for them and was paid well but wanted to get out of it, as he had found out the real gang behind the crimes.

He said he was working with some Finns and Latvians, but the actual control sat with an organisation in Saint Petersburg, Russia. He mentioned a name, Hemmo, as the Finn who told him this. Ari, smelling the possibility of money, began to frequent the harbour areas. After all, there were always bikes to be stolen as well.

Jussi nodded, realising now why some bikes had been stolen from waterfront locations.

Ari then explained that his friend had suddenly disappeared and stopped visiting the bar. Then, he found out that his friend's body had been recovered from a boat. Apparently, he was the one who had been shot and left for dead.

"Okay, we're getting somewhere now. You mentioned your

friend had found out the real plan; what do you mean?" Stefan asked.

Jussi leaned forward with interest.

Ari continued, "Well, he wouldn't tell me much about that. He only told me that he knew a Russian organisation was behind it, and their aim was to bring other criminal ventures to Finland."

They continued for another two hours, breaking for coffee and sandwiches at one stage. Ari kept talking, and Jussi and Stefan kept digging for more details.

After a while, it was clear there was nothing more to be extracted from Ari; they had all the available information. They concluded the interview, released Ari back to his cell and thanked Mirka, who left for home.

Jussi and Stefan discussed the interview at length, after which Jussi returned to the office. He briefed Tapio, who had arrived at the station during the interview, and together they updated the file. Subsequently, Jussi and Tapio used an empty office to call the Detective Inspector and update him on the news. Pekka decided that after writing up the file, they should finish for the day and get some rest. They would begin the hunt for the mysterious Hemmo the following morning.

Jussi and Tapio departed for home. On the way back, on the train, Jussi called Selma; she didn't answer but returned a short message that she was in the gym and would call him later.

It was a fine evening, with the sun still bearing down on Helsinki, giving rise to a balmy 21 degrees warmth. On another day, he might have gone kayaking, but after the recent attack, its attraction had worn off somewhat, and he didn't feel like doing it. Instead, he visited the Delicatessen in a local department store, bought a gourmet TV dinner to enjoy, and kicked back on his sofa. He had a feeling the days ahead would be busy.

TO MARIEHAMN

Jussi was right; the next day saw several more of the team placed on the hunt for the mysterious Hemmo. One officer searched for someone of that name on the convictions list from the past ten years to check if he had a criminal record. Another officer studied the population register to determine how many people of that name were registered as living in Helsinki. A further officer inspected the ports and airports data-bank for any evidence of movement. They had decided not to contact any potential informants aside from Ari because they didn't want to alert the criminals concerned.

Jussi's task was to research the list of people identified as possible leads. During the day, he reviewed several possible suspects, including some living elsewhere. One particular name stood out, and Jussi had a strong feeling that it could be him.

The 'Hemmo' in question lived in Malmi, Helsinki. He had spent two years in prison for handling stolen goods, and the file noted charges of theft and assault, although unproven. He had undertaken several international trips across the year, including Riga, Stockholm, Copenhagen and Travemünde in Germany. At this particular time, he was in Mariehamn, the principal city of the Åland Islands.

The team agreed there was a strong possibility of this 'Hemmo' being this suspect. They sat down at the conference table in the afternoon to discuss the next steps. After facts were laid out on the table, Pekka delivered his conclusion.

"It looks like a visit to Mariehamn is in order. Tapio and Jussi will fly there tonight. There'll be two objectives: firstly, we'll send a message to the local police this afternoon; however, a local briefing will also be necessary; secondly, we will apprehend Hemmo and any other party working with him. This action will prevent such crimes in Åland and hopefully lead us to the next person in the chain. Then we can start working with the Latvian police on something more concrete. It would be useful to get more uniform support for this, but I'm not sure if our colleagues in Mariehamn will have enough resources. You should take two more officers and get packing. Looking at the flight schedule, you could leave within two hours."

Jussi asked if he could take Stefan, who had been invaluable during the interview process. Pekka approved, subject to a discussion with Stefan's superior. A female officer named Leila was also recommended. After the team assembled, the four of them set off to their respective homes to pack lightly and prepare for travel to the Åland Islands.

◆ ◆ ◆

The weather was dreadful that evening, and none of the team enjoyed the flight across the Baltic Sea to Åland. The turbulence in the small turbo-prop plane had been uncomfortable, and the team struggled off the aircraft on arrival at the small airport.

With the driving rain outside, they were relieved to reach the hotel, a short taxi ride away. They agreed to drop their bags and meet for dinner in an hour.

Jussi found the hotel full of character and looked out of his small attic room across the ocean, with rain pattering on the skylight window. He hung a couple of shirts up in the wardrobe, as he expected to be there for at least two nights. After a quick freshen-up, he made for the bar where he found Tapio sitting silently, fondly cradling a malt whisky.

"This is what I need after that crossing. God above, I wasn't expecting that!" Tapio exclaimed.

"Yes, not exactly summer weather, was it? But we're here now. Let's relax this evening and start early tomorrow," replied Jussi.

The others joined a few minutes later and soon found themselves to be enjoying each other's company. A round of whiskies (gin and tonic for Leila) expedited this. Next, they moved to a table and ordered some burgers from the menu, together with another round of drinks. There were other people in the dining room, so the team deliberately avoided topics related to police work, especially the case in question.

Jussi viewed his colleagues and felt that this team was ideal for the task at hand. Neither Jussi nor Tapio had met Leila before but found her genuine, direct, and with a great sense of humour. She was a career police officer who had spent almost fifteen years in the force. She was in her late thirties but looked younger due to her size. With tied back blonde hair and a wicked laugh, she fitted in well with the rest of the team.

After an entertaining night, they all retired to bed, with the agreement that they would meet for breakfast at 7 am. Despite the howling wind and driving rain outside, Jussi slept like a log that night.

◆ ◆ ◆

The team was pleased to find the storm had broken in the morning and that sun was shining on Åland.

They took over a small, bright anteroom with a bay view and pushed a couple of tables together to create a meeting room.

After sitting down with their selections from the buffet table, they started to eat and discuss their plan of attack.

"Okay, so let's split up into two teams today," began Tapio. "I want us to stay in pairs at all times; Jussi has already been attacked once, and I don't want any of us to repeat the experience. I'll meet the local team shortly with Leila and brief them on the situation. We'll also research passenger arrivals and hotels in the area. Hopefully, we can locate where our suspect is staying. Then we'll check likely spots outside the city and around the island, which may contain the type of boats we're searching for. Let's meet for lunch at 1 pm to discuss next steps. Jussi, are you all set with your team?"

"Yes," replied Jussi. "Stefan and I will get straight down to the business of surveying the main harbour. Under the pretext of bringing a boat here to dock, we will check the boat and people traffic in the area. We have photos of the potential suspect, so we'll use them to identify him if he's around. If we see him, we'll contact you immediately for back-up and inform the local police."

"Great. We'll probably head to Hemmo's accommodation in the afternoon, providing we've confirmed that he's there. We need to remember that we don't have any clear evidence he's involved in anything yet. We may find some circumstantial stuff, but that won't be good enough to threaten him with at this stage. We need to catch him in the act or with sufficient evidence on his person. Neither of these will be easy. See you later."

Tapio and Leila left the table while Jussi and Stefan drained their coffees.

Rental cars had been pre-arranged, and they collected the keys at the reception. They had decided it was better to use an anonymous rental car than anything connected with the local police. Jussi left Stefan to drive as he checked the map. Stefan started the car, and they soon arrived in a small car park by the harbour.

The area was beautiful, and Jussi liked it at once. There was a marina with plenty of moored boats, varying from small rowing boats to a couple of enormous and undoubtedly costly motor yachts. Jussi whistled through his teeth as he looked at one.

"That would be some prize for a thief; it must be worth millions", Stefan commented.

"Although a little too big to hide anywhere?" Jussi added with a smile.

Stefan nodded in agreement.

They found the Harbour Master in an office nearby. They introduced themselves and explained that they wished to inquire about mooring a boat here, as they planned to spend some time here on business. Jussi asked some questions about the marina, how it worked, and the weather conditions in the area. He specified the type of boat and looked around for a place where this type of vessel could be moored.

Stefan monitored the area continually as he lit a cigarette and loitered around the office.

After sitting at a small café overlooking the marina, they checked some of the other mooring areas; there were several gangways off to the side of the main pier. They strolled up and down them, only returning to the café for a check-in call with the others.

Jussi called out, "Hey Tapio, it's all quiet here, and according to the Harbour Master, it's secure enough. Apparently, there's never been a boat theft in Mariehamn."

Tapio replied. "We've discovered some interesting information here. It seems the suspect used his real name to travel here and arrived a couple of days ago. He's staying at a hotel close to ours. A second ticket was booked on the same credit card belonging to someone called Samuli. We've asked them to check the name in Helsinki. So, now we know who they are and where they're staying."

"Right, so they must be on the job. Why else would they come here for a few days? Unless they think they deserve a vacation after their hard work?" Jussi joked.

"I suggest that two of us transfer to that hotel and the other two check out the possible locations where they may steal a boat," Tapio proposed.

"My money is on the main harbour at this stage. It looks so easy; why bother going to a remote area?" commented Stefan.

"How about if one of us stakes out the harbour area and the other takes the car and checks the other locations?" Suggested Leila.

"Good idea Leila," Tapio commented. "However, we need to stay in pairs. Remember, these men are dangerous and quite possibly armed; we can't take any risks. Besides, if we stake out their hotel well enough, we'll know their movements anyway."

They discussed the plan further and decided Jussi and Leila would become a couple and move to a double suite in the suspects' hotel for appearance's sake. This plan would allow them to keep tabs on them. Meanwhile, Tapio and Stefan would check out the other possible targets on the island during the afternoon. On the way, Tapio would call and brief the local police should they need some support.

As planned, Jussi and Leila moved into the hotel in the afternoon. They had secured a small suite with a bed and a sofa, which felt more appropriate. After moving their belongings into the room, they settled down for a long lunch in the restaurant.

They chose a table where Jussi would have a good view through the glass of the dining area, lounge and reception. This position would also allow Leila to watch the outside of the hotel.

Jussi was beginning his salad appetiser when two men walked in. He immediately recognised one of them as the suspect Hemmo from his photograph. He caught Leila's eye and began talking about the salad dressing. She immediately understood and deliberately didn't turn around but started to smile and nod.

Hemmo and Samuli had already spent two days at the hotel. They now had sufficient knowledge of the area to steal one of the boats in the harbour. They had planned to do it later that evening, so there was nothing to do today except relax. They ordered a bottle of wine and some steak with fries and thoroughly enjoyed their lunch. They had decided to treat these days as a working holiday. After all, they had plenty of money to spend these days, so they may as well enjoy themselves.

After the meal, Hemmo ordered coffees and cognacs, and they clinked glasses and drained them before returning to the hotel lift. Jussi observed them. He couldn't quite make out what they were saying but did hear the words 'To Success' as they clinked their glasses in a celebratory toast. Jussi had the feeling that a crime was imminent.

"They must have gone to their room to sleep off their lunch," Jussi commented to Leila as the pair disappeared inside the lift.

Leila nodded.

He continued, "Let's take turns to spend time down here. I'm guessing it will be late this evening when they act; if it takes place today, that is. Let's buy some magazines, use laptops, drink coffee and whatever else we can think of to allay suspicion. At the same time, one of us can loiter in the lounge. I'll check the back door to see if they could use that."

Jussi went upstairs to call Tapio. Then, they spent the afternoon exchanging places every couple of hours. Neither of them noticed any sign of the men and decided to make reservations for dinner. They had checked with the hotel manager, who, after showing their identification, informed them that the men had made reservations for dinner that evening at 7 pm. They made their reservation fifteen minutes earlier to be in the dining room when the suspects arrived.

By this time, Tapio and Stefan had returned from their scouting trip, armed with information and photographs about the other possible targets. They agreed with Jussi that the main harbour would be the target and decided not to divide their resources. Instead, they would stake out the pier whilst Jussi and Leila staked out the suspects. The trap was ready. The only thing remaining was the question: Would they act tonight?

◆ ◆ ◆

That evening, the two suspects entered the dining room according to plan. Jussi and Leila had changed clothes and chosen a different table. There were also a few more diners tonight, so they didn't feel too conspicuous. They had a bottle of wine on the table and laughed at one another's jokes to blend in with everyone else. Leila reported that the men seemed more serious tonight, although they again ate a hearty meal, this time without alcohol. They guessed that this was to keep their wits sharp for the activity ahead. The men lingered over coffee and headed up to their rooms a little before 10 pm.

Jussi and Leila ordered coffees and sat in reception. Jussi called and briefed Tapio and Stefan, who settled in the Harbour Master's office, watching through the windows. There were also three local uniformed officers prepared to assist, in a car, some distance away.

At 10.45 pm, the two suspects walked to the reception desk with bags and paid their bills. They told the girl behind the desk that they had to leave early due to a trip they were taking and left it at that.

They left the hotel and headed in the direction of the harbour. Jussi and Leila slowly stood up and put their coats on, heading out of the door at a leisurely pace. They stood outside the hotel for a moment and carefully watched the men turn the corner leading to the seafront. They slowly walked and linked arms as they wished to appear as a loving couple, simply enjoying the night air.

By this time, Tapio and Stefan had their guns on the table, ready to leave the hut at a moment's notice. Hemmo and Samuli walked purposefully towards the harbour and made their way towards their pre-chosen vessel. They had already called ahead, and Edgars' fishing boat was almost within reach. They were content as they had enjoyed their time on the island, the wind had died down, and they could see another profitable trip ahead of them.

Thanks to their informant in Helsinki, the criminals were utterly unaware of the net closing in on them. The suspects calmly boarded the boat, and Samuli got straight to work on the electrics while Hemmo stowed the bags.

"Now, now, now!" shouted Tapio into his phone.

As Jussi and Leila ran towards the boat, Tapio and Stefan leapt out of the hut and ran in the other direction. The local police car also started along the street and appeared at the corner.

Hemmo and Samuli had been so busy preparing to leave that they hadn't seen anyone until Hemmo cast a glance down the gangway and saw the group running towards them. He instinctively grabbed his pistol, swerved around and started shooting. Samuli began to the engine; however, he was too late.

Jussi and Leila were in front of the group and drew their weapons. A stray bullet caught Leila in the shoulder, and she hit the wooden deck hard. Jussi knelt and shot three times into Hemmo, who fell backwards into the boat. Samuli turned around to see what was happening. He realised that he didn't have a chance to escape without loosening the ropes and so limply raised his hands as the boat strained against its mooring.

Jussi stood covering Samuli as Stefan pulled him roughly out of the cockpit. Simultaneously, Tapio jumped in to switch the engine off to and check on Hemmo. Jussi ran back to Leila, who was staggering towards them. He was relieved to note that she seemed to have suffered only a light flesh wound and took off his jacket to wrap it around her shoulder. An ambulance arrived soon afterwards, pronouncing Hemmo dead and taking Leila away for treatment. The police took Samuli straight to a police cell - it had all been over in seconds.

Following the excitement, the team went to the station to drink hot coffee and eat doughnuts. The arrest had been challenging, though, and they hadn't intended anyone to get hurt, especially Leila. Hemmo's death was also a blow; however, they had one of the men to question.

After they had finished their refreshments and let the suspect sweat in the cells, Jussi and Tapio went to interview him.

Samuli was sitting at a table, shackled in handcuffs, with a sour expression on his face - often earned by hardened criminals. The report from Helsinki had described him as such, as he had seen involvement in theft, assault, criminal damage and attempted murder. Now, he was suspected of much more. Unfortunately, Hemmo had been the intelligent one. The team was now apprehensive about managing Samuli to provide any tangible information.

"Good evening Samuli, would you like some coffee?" Tapio asked as he sat down.

Samuli grunted affirmatively, as Jussi handed him a paper

cup he had brought in. There was no gratitude.

"You've been busy, haven't you, Samuli," said Jussi. "We have a whole list of charges against you, including theft, criminal damage, assault, murder, attempted murder, and the list goes on and on. I would be willing to bet that you won't see the outside of a prison cell for the rest of your life."

Samuli looked at him and grunted again. He was staring at the coffee inside his cup and swirling it around in thought.

"Now that Hemmo is no longer with us, all of the blame will fall on you. That's a shame," said Tapio.

As Jussi observed Samuli, Tapio continued, "Although, I think you were just doing your job, right? It really would be a shame if you had to take responsibility for everything. I wonder if you might possess any information that could lead us to the real person in charge? That way, I imagine your sentence could be a little shorter?"

Samuli broke his silence. "Do you know what would happen to me if I told you anything?"

Jussi looked at Tapio; he had been here before, with the bike thief. Only this interview looked as if it could be much more beneficial.

"What if we could guarantee your safety?" Tapio asked.

"You can't guarantee anything. I wouldn't stand a chance, and I would be dead within days," Samuli replied, looking at his coffee cup again.

"What if we could offer you some kind of a deal?" Tapio suggested.

He let that thought marinate for a few moments.

"What kind of deal?" Samuli asked.

"Look, Samuli," Jussi said, placing his head on his hands. We know that you've been taking the boats to Latvia, and we know that the real boss of this operation is in Saint Petersburg."

At this revelation, Samuli's eyes opened wider as he didn't realise the police knew so much. He shifted his position and sat up straighter.

"Really?" he said. "Please tell me where you heard this fascinating story?"

"We never reveal our sources Samuli. It is correct, though, isn't it?" asked Tapio, leaning back in his chair.

No answer.

"Look, Samuli, if you aren't interested in working with us, we can hand this matter over, bring a lawyer here, and begin the criminal charges. The next time I will see you will be to testify against you in court," Jussi stated, with some malice in his voice.

He was pretty confident that the man sitting in front of him was the one who had rammed his kayak in Helsinki.

"What kind of deal could we make?" Samuli repeated.

They continued with a similar approach as they had taken with Ari, the bike thief. This time, there was no hesitation. Samuli could guess he would spend the rest of his life in prison if he didn't do something now. He was particularly interested when offered a deal to settle him in a minimum-security prison in the countryside, with no dangerous gang members posing a threat to him. When he heard they could work on the charges to bring them down by as much as half, he was keen to discuss it further.

"Right, I can tell you what I know in return for that," he said. "We take the boats across the Baltic sea to meet a fishing boat. That vessel is designed to lift and store the boat while we board and travel to Latvia. We go to a small place just west of Riga. Then, the boats are usually broken down and shipped to Saint Petersburg."

"Can you show us exactly where?" Jussi asked.

"Yes, as soon as I have your deal in writing," Samuli replied.

"Tell us about the Latvians first - then we can talk about the Russians," directed Tapio.

Samuli proceeded to tell them about the contact in Riga, with no name yet. He explained the man had others working for him, as there were other criminal activities in Latvia. He knew little about Russia, only that the Russian bosses belonged to a crime syndicate, expanding country by country, eyeing Finland as their next target.

The detectives extracted as much information as possible and contacted Pekka in Helsinki to discuss next steps and obtain an offer in writing. Samuli was the second criminal prepared to give up others in exchange for a more comfortable ride.

Jussi and Tapio stood in the hallway and took some water from the cooler.

"Honor amongst thieves is not very common these days," remarked Tapio.

Stefan joined them. "What a result!" he exclaimed after they briefed him.

"This is going to lead us to the Latvian organisation." "And from there, to Saint Petersburg!" replied Jussi.

"Let's hope we don't have to go there, though; that would seem like a step into the lion's den," Tapio commented.

The others nodded in agreement. Jussi was delighted. He could already see a potential victory ahead, confirming his detective position and possibly promotion. His direction was clear, and he would push to lead the way forward overseas.

The team spent the following day in Mariehamn in a long meeting, making plans and arrangements. They also visited Leila at the hospital, who was now comfortable.

That evening, they took a small private plane back to Helsinki. They managed to contain the press in Mariehamn and were keen to avoid any publicity that might damage any deal with Samuli. They were also pleased that Leila would return to Helsinki after a couple of days.

Later that night, they arrived at Vantaa airport, where they picked up the cars and drove to the station in Helsinki. The chase was set to continue.

THE HIDEOUT

The Witness Protection Department in Helsinki took over handling the suspects involved in the bike and boat thefts. Now, the task force's primary role was to follow the trail back to Riga and work with the Latvian police to close the noose on the operation there.

Having already visited Riga and established a good relationship with its police force, Jussi was appointed liaison. At the same time, Tapio would run the overall operation from Helsinki.

On request, Stefan had been assigned to Jussi once more, and they made arrangements to fly to Riga that morning. Their objective was to ensure the close cooperation of the Latvian Police Force and determine the location of the gang's base of operations.

Jussi knew the Latvian connection may have already changed their plans following the no-show of Hemmo and Samuli. He hoped they would think the fault lay with the two Finns having a navigation problem and return to Riga to await news rather than suspect any police involvement.

Edgars was furious.

The fishing boat had made the voyage to the appointed location and waited two hours past the planned arrival time. Eventually, Edgars had directed his men to haul anchor and point the boat back towards Riga. It had been a completely wasted trip.

Have those idiots got lost, or has something else happened?

Edgars couldn't raise Hemmo on his mobile phone at all. Whatever the case, he was not waiting to find out. He decided to return to base and await news. It would take much of the night to travel back, and no doubt his Russian colleagues would not be happy about an entire week without any new boats.

He fumed silently on the bridge on the return trip, eventually going below deck to get a few hours' sleep while the fishing boat sailed on into the night.

◆ ◆ ◆

Jussi and Stefan arrived at the airport in Riga. It was raining, and the scene was grey as they landed. Due to the urgency, a private plane had been arranged, and they made the trip in less than forty-five minutes.

On arrival, Jussi was pleased to see Janis as he met them at the airport and whisked them away in a black Mercedes towards the city. They called the Chief of Police in Riga during the drive and briefed him. The Chief assured them that they would have the use of a conference room and any assistance required to research possible locations. In addition, and if necessary, he promised the support of the Latvian OMEGA squad: the heavily armed unit tasked to fight organised crime and counter-terrorism.

When they arrived at the police station, a smiling officer named Helena met them and showed them directly to a meeting room. She was a colleague of Janis and would support them on logistics. Also present was a Sergeant, wearing a paramilitary uniform, who introduced himself simply as Alberts, from OMEGA. They sat down over coffee and pastries and discussed the plan.

Samuli had eventually described the base of operations for the boat thefts, and Alberts provided some possible names and photos of Edgars. Now they could make real progress. Helena set about providing potential addresses in Latvia for Edgars. Alberts knew that if he were who he thought he was: Edgars Kalnina, this would be a good catch, as he was known to be running criminal activities within the country. Alberts also said that Edgars had a hands-on approach and trusted very few people, maintaining a small but effective organisation. However, he was also suspected to be linked to a larger organisation in Russia, called the Vipers.

The next step was to determine the location. If the police could do that, they could simply wait for the criminals to arrive. Alberts would have his team standing by, and Jussi would go with Stefan and Janis to meet with the marine police to work their way over to the area by boat. OMEGA would only be called in when they found the exact location. Helena would become the single point of contact for the Latvian police and Tapio for the team in Helsinki, as the offshore mobile reception would be poor.

The team left for the harbour. The vessel that awaited them was imposing: a powerful jet boat with huge outboard motors attached to the rear. This boat was unmarked, but another was adjacent, with police markings. Janis explained that they would go in the unmarked one while the other stood by at a safe distance.

"Well, if it comes down to a chase, we'll certainly catch them in this!" Jussi smiled.

Everyone nodded as they took their seats, and the boat opened its throttle. There would be no talking on the way due to the overpowering noise from the engines.

❖ ❖ ❖

Edgars awoke to the sound of his mobile phone alarm and grudgingly got up from his bunk. He was beginning to wonder why he still took part in these operations directly. Although, his opinion was usually that some of his men were still not smart enough to make the right decisions and would probably screw things up.

Perhaps when I find the right person? he thought.

However, for the moment, he would continue to lead things here. He climbed the ladder to the wheelhouse, nodded to two of his men who were looking ahead, and poured himself a thick black coffee. The morning was light now as the sun had finally cut through the drizzle to illuminate the coast ahead.

"How long?" Edgars asked.

The man at the wheel informed him it would take another hour. Edgars returned to his cabin with the coffee and scanned his phone for news from Mariehamn, but there was still nothing - he sighed in frustration.

◆ ◆ ◆

Jussi and the team soon reached Jurmula in the powerful boat, continuing further west. According to Samuli, the likely location was only a couple of kilometres from there, and they would reach it in minutes.

After the sandy beach of Jurmala, the shoreline was mainly rocky, surrounded by tall trees. Jussi thought it looked like Finland, noting some wooden cottages that looked out to sea. They turned around a corner and saw a small bay. Looking at it through powerful binoculars, he could see a gravel beach and a large old boathouse. There were also some other outbuildings nearby. The area looked precisely as Samuli had described. Jussi took a short video clip, which he sent to Helena and Tapio.

The boat stopped and idled, awaiting confirmation of the location. A few minutes later, Jussi received a message to the affirmative and waved the vessel to continue onwards. Janis called Alberts to proceed with his team, waiting in their powerful black SUVs on Riga's outskirts.

On receiving the signal, the three trucks started their engines and sped off in the direction of Jurmala. If Jussi could have seen the firepower, he would have been impressed. The team carried machine guns, shotguns and sniper rifles, together with handguns attached to each officer's belt. Things were not going to go quietly.

As the minutes passed, everyone awaited the signal, while a helicopter took to the skies, high above, to try and spot the fishing vessel as it closed in on the bay. It didn't take long, and everyone stood down to allow the fishing boat time to approach and tie up to the long concrete pier.

Then, suddenly, the operation began.

"Go! Go! Go!" yelled Janis.

The speed boat powered up and violently surged ahead. Simultaneously, the waiting SUVs began to drive toward the outbuildings at speed. The second police boat and helicopter roared into view from behind and above. Two men were waiting in the house, and they were shocked by the sheer force of the attack. They took one look at the number of officers surrounding them and walked outside with their hands in the air. They were quickly pushed to the floor, heads down, handcuffed and frisked.

The fishing vessel was a different story. On the approach of Jussi's boat, machine-gun fire began and peppered the water around them. Everyone dived downwards in the police boats.

In the fishing boat, Edgars ran to the wheelhouse and barked orders to turn due west with all speed. He told his men to fire at anything approaching and telephoned for his car to meet them.

There were seven men in total on the fishing trawler. The noise was deafening, with most firing at the boat or into the air towards the helicopter. Janis had to steer the police boat away due to the ferocity of the fire. OMEGA had targeted the fishing vessel with sniper rifles from the beach, and bullets tore into its wooden hull.

"Faster, faster," shouted Edgars.

The fishing boat, having no cargo, built up speed. As yet, due to the swell of the waves and the distances involved, nobody from either side had received a bullet.

Alberts from OMEGA directed two vehicles to follow the boat's direction from the coast road. One group of officers remained to secure the base and the men they had arrested. The OMEGA SUVs almost flew along the dirt road and swerved onto the main road, immediately accelerating forward.

Jussi's boat and the other police boat were following the vessel. Janis saw no point in risking any injuries, so they remained a safe distance behind, tracking their route and updating OMEGA as they did so. The sound of a helicopter cut through the noise of their engines as it did the same thing, overhead. Jussi wondered how the gang could hope to escape, but it seemed they were determined to try.

◆ ◆ ◆

Back in Helsinki, the conference table was surrounded by several team members now, anxiously waiting for LIVE updates on the action. It seemed they now had the Latvian connection within their grasp.

The fishing trawler had probably never been pushed to its

limits before. It was now cruising at a steady fourteen knots, heading east in the direction of the port city of Ventspils. The powerful police launches could quickly have overtaken it; however, the team was mindful of the weapons on board. The fishing boat also offered superior defensive positions when compared to the open-cockpit speed boats.

They continued for another twenty minutes like this, with no real progress. Jussi was becoming impatient. As the boat's bow cut through the waves, it continually threw cold water over his face. It had also started to drizzle, and the sky was looking grey, affecting their visibility.

Suddenly, there was a flurry of gunfire from the boat without warning, and they had to pull back a little more. Jussi tried to peer through the rain and see what was going on. The helicopter radioed down to the boat, and Janis leaned over to translate, shouting at the top of his voice.

"The chopper can see something happening. It looks like they're dropping a dinghy over the side. It could be time to act. I am going to update OMEGA."

Now, peering carefully, Jussi could make out something himself. A launch was dropped over the side, and an outboard motor had fired up. Two occupants were inside as it started to move towards the shore. At the same time, on the horizon, a large, grey military-looking vessel was approaching - Janis had called in the big guns. The fishing vessel then dropped another dinghy, and more men climbed aboard. They started the engine and headed towards a small inlet.

The helicopter was directly overhead by this time, and the speedboats were accelerating towards the shore. The gang started firing again. The Latvian police had decided enough was enough at this stage, and they opened fire on the small boats. They hit two gang members, the remainder of which soon raised their hands.

Jussi's boat powered towards the shore, pursuing the first dinghy, while the other police launch met the second one, which subsequently surrendered. Meanwhile, the two men jumped out, abandoned the first dinghy and waded to the shore. Jussi's launch accelerated, ready to slow down as soon as they reached shallow water to allow Jussi and Janis to jump into the surf.

"Stay here and cover us, just in case," Jussi directed Stefan.

Stefan aimed his weapon as straight as he could, considering the continuous movement of the boat, and aimed at the two men running up the beach.

At the other side of the forest, half of the OMEGA team stayed with the SUVs and were staking out the road. They guessed that the fugitives would arrange a pick-up by car as it was their only visible means of escape. The rest of the OMEGA team picked their way slowly through the forest, with guns raised, hoping to meet the fugitives running the other way.

At this point, Edgars and his bodyguard, Karlis, were cutting through the forest at speed. They had a destination clearly in mind. Edgars had used the small harbour as a base of operations for many of his criminal activities over the years and had prepared for the eventuality of discovery. Surrounding the area were several small bunkers, each containing some means of escape.

The first bunker was near the shoreline and contained a small dinghy with an outboard motor. Edgars had already discounted this as being a waste of time. More bunkers held small caches of weapons and trail motorcycles. The third bunker in the centre was concealed entirely and, in addition to firearms, contained food and drink for several days. This bunker was their destination.

Edgars decided that they wouldn't stand much chance trying to escape from this heavy force, so they should make for the concealed bunker and disappear.

Karlis, his bodyguard, pointed out the landmark first. It was a large rock, and they made for it as fast as possible. Behind the rock, they slid across a heavy flat rock to reveal a metal trapdoor. They opened it and climbed down a narrow ladder, switching on a single lightbulb as they did so. Edgars pulled the handle that slid the rock back into place again. Karlis secured the locking mechanism, and they dropped down onto the ground, taking two machine pistols from a cabinet, placing them on the table in readiness. Edgars also took a bottle of vodka from on top of a filing cabinet, and they pulled up some folding camp chairs. He set two glasses on the table and filled them to the brim.

"That was close. Too close," Edgars remarked.

He raised his glass to Karlis, who did the same and took a drink. They felt safe for the moment, and both heaved a sigh of relief.

At ground level, activity was high. Jussi and his colleagues stalked carefully through the undergrowth, periodically searching and pointing their guns. They heard a rustle from the trees in front and suddenly found guns pointed at their heads. It was OMEGA who lowered their weapons when they recognized them.

"Where the hell did they disappear to?" Jussi asked aloud.

The team continued searching, supported by more uniformed police, who arrived with Sirens blaring. Shortly afterwards, one of the OMEGA squad discovered one of the bunkers. The team decided that the fugitives could have used trail bikes to escape, and they swiftly erected roadblocks in all directions.
Meanwhile, the helicopter returned and conducted a search over the forest in case the suspects had made their escape across country.

Edgars and his associate were now on the run.

◆ ◆ ◆

Back at the harbour, while searching through the old house, officers discovered interesting evidence: papers which included maps and documents relating to various boats. There was also a vessel halfway to being taken apart. They were pleased when this vessel was found to be an exact match for the most recent theft from Helsinki.

As they looked, they found many other boat parts scattered around the top floor of the house, neatly laid out, like a warehouse. It was undoubtedly the place. They had recovered the converted fishing boat, and some of Edgars' men were under arrest. The only problem was, where was their leader?

◆ ◆ ◆

That evening, back at the hotel, Jussi and Stefan spent time writing up the day's events. After this, they briefed the team in Helsinki, many of whom were working late to support the operation. The Finnish police maintained close communication with the Latvians throughout, sharing information freely.

OMEGA had also raided Edgars' main home and office. It seemed much of the police force of Riga were involved in what had become one of the most significant investigations and manhunts in their history. Edgars was engaged in many suspected crimes, and the new evidence arising was just what the Latvian police had been waiting for.

Back in the forest, the police staked out where the fugitives had disappeared. Janis promised to call Jussi and Stefan if and when they were apprehended.

It was late that night when Jussi's head hit the pillow. He

was relieved that the day was over and lying on his bed in his hotel room; he couldn't help thinking how far away he felt from Rauma.

◆ ◆ ◆

In Saint Petersburg, the atmosphere was tense.

Gregor smashed his phone down on the table and glared at his assistant. He had received a message from one of Edgars' men that the police had raided the Latvian base of operations, together with Edgars' home and office. Apparently, Edgars was nowhere to be found. Gregor called for an urgent conference call between his executives.

"Who the hell has done this? How can they take down our Latvian operation in a day?" Gregor asked with a mix of anger and disbelief. "Someone has talked! Some snivelling, little wretch has talked. I'm going to find them, and I'll take them apart with my bare hands. I want the names of the key police investigators in this mess as well. I'm not giving Latvia up. We need to establish a new base and continue our activities, with or without Edgars. Let's make a plan tomorrow. Get everyone here at 1 pm to discuss this face to face. I also want all the information we can find out about this mess so we know where we stand."

The activity level was high in Saint Petersburg that night.

SAINT PETERSBURG

Jussi awoke the following day and stretched. There had been some tense moments over the past couple of days, but he was delighted progress had been made in the case.

He checked his phone to see if there had been a message from Janis concerning the missing fugitives, but there was no message. He did note an email stating that Stefan was to return to Helsinki. That same message instructed Jussi to stay as long as necessary, continuing to be the on-site liaison between Finland and Latvia.

He got himself ready for the day and made for the restaurant downstairs for breakfast. He was hungry as he had eaten little the day before.

When he arrived, he saw Janis, who waved him over. He was already enjoying a hearty breakfast.

"I thought I'd come and meet you this morning," Janis said. "Besides, your breakfast is much better than mine," he grinned.

"I'm pleased you did," Jussi returned the smile.

He poured a glass of orange juice, a bowl of muesli and took a seat, ordering coffee from a waiter as he did so.

"How's the cooked breakfast?" Jussi asked, gesturing at Janis's plateful.

"Not bad, thanks; it's better than my usual bad coffee and biscuits anyway," Janis replied.

Jussi laughed. Cops were the same everywhere.

Janis proceeded to update Jussi on any details he may have missed from the preceding day's activity. The manhunt was still underway for Edgars, and OMEGA was combing the area to locate him. He told Jussi that the second man was Edgars' known personal bodyguard. Jussi had more questions and was especially interested in whether information had surfaced concerning the Russian angle.

"We found papers relating to sales and distribution, made with a company called: Plamya Feniksa."

Jussi looked up inquiringly.

"Flames of the Phoenix", Janis interpreted. "This is the company that purchased marine and mechanical parts, presumably rebuilt and subsequently resold. We're trying to find out more about the company but believe it was just a front for importing the stolen boat parts. There seems to be a lucrative market around the Black Sea.

Jussi nodded.

"Any more names in Russia yet?" he asked.

Janis replied, "Not apart from Gregor. It seems the organisation in Latvia was quite independent. They will have made some mistakes, but we need to be careful, as if they suspect we know any names, they may go to ground."

"So, how do we go forward?" Jussi inquired.

"First, we need to finish extracting all the information," Janis answered. "Then, we will put together a plan and start talking to the Russian authorities, probably the Interior Ministry. With their cooperation, I hope we'll be able to locate the suspects and bring them into custody. With the number of people under arrest right now, I'm sure OMEGA can extract plenty of useful information."

Janis leaned back, apparently quite confident of a result.

Just as Jussi was pouring a second coffee, Janis's phone rang. He answered the caller with a succession of affirmatives.

"That's it!" he exclaimed at the end of the conversation.

"What?" Jussi asked in anticipation.

"One of the men we arrested from the base has talked and given the person's name at the top of all this: Gregor Ivanov from Saint Petersburg. A conference call has been arranged with the Chief of Police in Moscow in one hour. We need to get to the office."

"How did they get him to talk so fast? Isn't he afraid as well?" Jussi asked.

"I wouldn't ask," Janis answered, raising his eyebrows.

The detectives quickly finished their breakfast and left the hotel. Janis's car was parked outside, so they drove to the office downtown.

When they arrived, Janis took Jussi to a large conference room, where half a dozen men were sitting around a large table. Introductions were made, and Jussi found himself sitting opposite the Chief of Police of Riga. Both he and Janis spoke fluent English, and the others seemed to understand well enough, so the conversation went smoothly. A large screen was switched on, and with a few clicks on a laptop, the conference room in Helsinki came into view. Jussi raised a hand by way of welcome to the task force members in Helsinki, who were all assembled.

The meeting was split in two. The first half was an information update by each side, although primarily from the Latvian angle due to the recent events. The second half of the meeting was a planning exercise on how to approach the situation in Russia.

Decisions were made. Firstly, a joint communication would be sent to Saint Petersburg, countersigned by their respective governments, from the Chiefs of Police in Helsinki and Riga. Next, they decided that Jussi and Janis would be the ambassadors to take this forward with the Russian police and Interior Ministry, both being familiar with the case. The message would be sent that day and provided cooperation was agreed; arrangements would be made for the detectives to fly to Russia the following day.

The team were aware they had already acquired some sound evidence and witnesses; however, this would only be enough to investigate in Russia, not to act. They would need to build a stronger case with more concrete facts. They also required Edgars to be in custody to interrogate him. In addition to this, and most importantly, they would need the Russian authorities' blessing and support - easier said than done. Gregor Ivanov was a well-known, wealthy and influential figure in Saint Petersburg who might have friends and contacts in high places.

The meeting took the whole morning. The afternoon was spent making arrangements and putting together the final dossier for the Russian Interior Ministry. The plane tickets were booked for Jussi and Janis, with a return date of one week, knowing that it may take this long to provide a detailed briefing and formulate an agreed plan. There was little more that could be done by early evening, and the meeting was adjourned.

◆ ◆ ◆

Jussi decided to visit a department store and purchase some essentials. He was running out of clothes, and it looked like he would need to survive another week on the road. He spent a couple of hours purchasing some new shirts and other essentials. Then, he took the opportunity to take a short walk around the old town to take in its beauty.

I should have brought my camera, Jussi thought to himself as he stood in the old town square looking at the buildings.

He spotted an Irish Pub on the corner of the square and wandered over to it. He took a seat at the bar and ordered steak pie and chips together with a beer. It was a perfect combination. He felt like relaxing for a couple of hours, without the constant conversation about the case going on around him.

After a couple of drinks and some food, he could get a good night's sleep before his flight in the morning. It was quiet in the pub and, he finished his meal in peace. He was about to order a second beer when someone arrived on the stool next to him.

"Hi, do you speak English?" she said.

Jussi looked at the voice's owner and saw a striking girl with red hair and penetrating eyes. She wore a green leather jacket with a matching green ribbon in her hair.

"Yes, I do," Jussi instinctively smiled at her.

The girl was very attractive and, at the same time, very distinctive.

She offered her hand by way of introduction.

"I'm Lucy."

"I'm Jussi. Where are you from?" he asked, detecting an accent.

"Limerick in Ireland," she replied with a smile. "What other kind of girl might you expect to find in an Irish bar?"

"Maybe Latvian? Or Russian?" he joked.

They laughed, and as the barman arrived, Jussi offered to buy Lucy a drink, to which she agreed and asked for a beer too.

During the conversation that followed, it turned out that Lucy had recently moved to Riga to study fashion and had only been there a couple of weeks. Jussi was quite happy to have some company this evening and something to take his mind off the case.

When asked his purpose in Riga, he replied that he was with the Finnish police and was on a public relations mission to increase cooperation with Latvia. She seemed impressed.

As they talked, she stared continuously into his eyes, hanging on his every word. Jussi was quite happy with this attention and its distraction from the day. He enjoyed himself, and several more drinks were ordered and consumed by both parties.

After a few hours, Jussi checked his watch and noted it was already 10.30 pm. He decided it was time to move. He still needed to pack, and although it was not a dawn flight, it was earlier than he would have liked, so he made his excuses.

"Okay. Would you mind if I walk with you?" Lucy asked.

Jussi thought for a moment, and something made him agree. They left the bar and strolled towards his hotel, her arm linked with his. Lucy made no move to leave. They walked into the lobby and onwards to the lift. Then she moved closer to him and opened her lips to kiss him. They did so, and the decision was made. They walked to his room and, after opening the door, began to remove each other's clothes and kiss. They made love noisily and laughed a lot.

Finally, they fell asleep in each other's arms.

◆ ◆ ◆

Jussi awoke the following day to the hotel phone ringing beside his bed. He remembered Lucy and noticed that she wasn't in bed next to him. He looked at the time on the alarm clock that read 6.36 am. He had meant to wake earlier and checked around the bedside table for his mobile phone. He couldn't find it anywhere and got up to walk to the bathroom. Lucy was gone. He looked around the room and began to search everywhere.

"On shit!" he exclaimed.

Suddenly, the thought ran through his head that he'd been robbed. He searched everywhere and found that his small credit card wallet was missing too. He walked quickly to the armchair where he'd hidden his main wallet under the cushion; thankfully it was still there. He would need to buy a temporary phone and stop his card at the bank.

Over the years, Jussi had acquired the habit of going out with only the basics; it was simple to stop one credit card if he lost his wallet. It seemed to have paid off this time. A quick check around the rest of the room determined that it appeared to be only those two items that were missing. He cursed himself for drinking so much and being so stupid as to be taken in by the girl. He quickly showered and dressed. Then, he made the necessary calls before leaving the hotel so he wouldn't need to explain anything to Janis. He would say that he'd lost his mobile phone and buy a temporary one at the airport.

It was a frustrated Jussi who went down for breakfast that morning.

After eating, Janis met him in the lobby and together, they drove to the airport. Jussi had been getting to like Riga, but Lucy, if that was her real name, had spoiled it, and he felt cheated by the city now.

Well, I could have been that stupid anywhere, he told himself. *Best to leave it behind him now.*

On arrival at the airport terminal, they checked in. The Latvian police had arranged business class tickets, so they made their way to the complimentary lounge. Jussi excused himself and bought a cheap phone from a kiosk on the way, planning to arrange a proper one on his return to Helsinki.

He arrived in the lounge and went straight to the coffee machine. After receiving a cappuccino, he made for the seating area, where Janis was on his mobile with his back turned. As he neared, he heard the last part of a conversation.

"......Yes, it's fine, no, he won't suspect anything and this can be closed down very soon."

Jussi stopped in his tracks and waited until Janis ended the call. He slowly returned to the breakfast bar and took a croissant from the plate. He busied himself there for a moment while some thoughts went through his mind.

Who was on the other end of that phone? Can I trust Janis? Should I confront him? Does he have something to do with all of this?

In the end, he decided he wouldn't mention anything about what he had heard but be wary of Janis from now on.

He arrived at the seating area with his snack and coffee and sat down.

"The office again!" Janis said, waving his mobile.

"I know the feeling," smiled Jussi.

They both used the waiting time to peer into their laptops and catch up with some emails.

After an hour, the flight departure flashed onto the screen, and they walked the short distance to the plane. The flight took less than an hour and a half, and although they exchanged conversation, they were both mainly concerned with the contents of their laptops. Jussi deliberately made small talk every now and then to mask his suspicions towards Janis. Still, as they both had work to do, not much effort was required.

On the way, Jussi found his thoughts wavering back to Selma

and then Heli. He told himself how stupid he was for allowing women such as Lucy and Heli to cause problems for him. He resolved to call Selma later.

On arrival, they walked down the gangway and waited a few minutes on the tarmac for the bus to arrive. A police car came, and after checking their identities, the occupants invited Jussi and Janis to join them. Their car proceeded directly to the downtown police station.

◆ ◆ ◆

Gregor sat in his private office at his desk. He used his main office for meetings, but this room was completely private and led off from his enormous bedroom walk-in closet. It was secure with a thick metal door, video camera and keypad entrance. It was also designed as a panic room, being practically impregnable from the outside.

The office was impressive and sparsely decorated in a modern style, with a unique desk fashioned from an aeroplane wing. The rest of the room was laid out with neat shiny white cupboards lining one side of the room and a fully stocked bar at the other. A large white rug was laid over oak floorboards in the middle of the room. There were also a couple of additional chairs, more for decoration, as no one else was ever invited here. This was where Gregor kept his innermost secrets and valuables.

As he was reading through some papers, his mobile phone rang. Unusually, he spent most of the call listening to the other party. The caller imparted information about the progress of the case in question. Gregor spent a couple of minutes listening and then instructed the caller to keep him informed.

After the telephone conversation, he took a sip from his coffee and smiled. It was helpful to have connections within the police force, expensive but sometimes essential. He had also been considering another course of action which he now decided upon. He picked up his phone and dialled.

"Natalja, I'm afraid that Edgars has now compromised our situation to an unacceptable level. Please take the necessary steps to remove him. I would like you to take over direct control of the Latvian operation: establish a new office and bring things back together so we can move on. Forget the boats for now. I have a new plan which we'll discuss when you are ready."

Gregor put the phone down. It was no longer the time for stealth. Now was the time for action.

❖ ❖ ❖

Selma put down her mobile phone. It was the fifth time over the past couple of days that she had attempted to reach Jussi, and now the number rang out yet again. If he had grown tired of her and found other interests, she would do the same and wouldn't call again. She sighed and picked up her gym bag from the sofa. If nothing else, this evening, Selma planned to turn her disappointment into positive energy for her workout. She walked out into the morning sun and made her way to her car and onwards to work.

❖ ❖ ❖

Jussi arrived at the Central Police Station in Saint Petersburg. It was an impressive sight: the enormous building hailed from a different era, with ornate sculptures decorating the façade. Dressed in pale pink, Jussi thought it seemed more like an art gallery than a police station. However, inside, it was a different matter. It was sparsely furnished, stark and almost sanitary.

They were led into a grand hallway and ushered into a large conference room. It contained one of the most enormous tables Jussi had ever seen, made from polished and expensive hardwood. Various flags were draped around the room, and a large painting of the president dominated one wall. A young female officer offered them coffee and water, who then left the room and closed the large double doors.

"This looks a bit more luxurious," Janis commented.

"This is probably where they receive guests. I imagine the rest of the building looks the same as the lobby."

Jussi nodded and drank some coffee, which he found pleasantly strong.

A couple of minutes later, a small delegation entered the room. They walked in with almost military precision. Jussi and Janis instinctively stood up and waited for them to near, offering a handshake as they did so.

Introductions were made, and the head of the group, Commander Pinchouk, sat down.

"Thank you for the dossier you sent me. It was most informative. Due to the gravity of the situation, the Interior Ministry has granted authorisation to proceed with this investigation. Up to this point, it has been rather complex due to the involvement of several different countries and their police authorities. However, the issue is here in Russia now, and we will assume control over the case. I ask that you debrief this team with any information you may have. Tonight, as gratitude from our country, I would like you to experience the fabulous city of Saint Petersburg. I will arrange for your return to your respective countries in the morning. Your governments have been informed, and Russia thanks you for your support."

After that short speech, he stood up from his chair, nodded and quickly strode out of the room.

Jussi and Janis were a little confused and looked at each other. It didn't seem appropriate to call the senior officer back, so they settled down to speak to the team assembled around the table.

During the next couple of hours, it became evident that their services would not be required in Russia on an operational basis. Therefore, they answered all the questions as requested and provided a verbal summary of each event, referencing the appropriate parts of the case file. Janis covered events in Latvia, and Jussi covered Finland and beyond. Lunch was brought into the room, comprising sandwiches, salads, fruit juice, coffee and pastries.

After lunch, they continued until they had nothing else to tell. Jussi considered keeping something back from time to time. Still, as their respective governments were involved, he decided not to risk it.

At precisely 3 pm, the meeting adjourned. They all shook hands, and the two detectives were escorted to a waiting car that took them straight to a hotel. The pair didn't discuss anything on the way, except small talk. They wondered if their conversation would be relayed back to the Russian authorities or even if it was being recorded. Only when they arrived in the hotel lobby did they feel free to talk once more.

"Wow, it seems they want to impress us!" exclaimed Janis, taking in his surroundings.

"Indeed," agreed Jussi, as they made their way to the reception desk.

The hotel was remarkably ornate and had massive chandeliers hanging from the ceiling, illuminating its gold decoration.

Jussi and Janis checked in, and the receptionist handed Jussi an envelope, which he opened.

"Well, look at this! We have a dinner reservation and tickets to the ballet for this evening's performance. The note says: with thanks from Russia."

"Nice!" Janis remarked, "What time?"

"A car will collect us at 6 pm," Jussi replied.

"Okay, let's catch up on a few things and meet here in a couple of hours, say at 5.45 pm?"

"Sounds good," Janis agreed.

They made their way to the lift and onwards to their respective rooms.

"Wow, I could get used to this!" Jussi exclaimed into thin air as he entered his room.

He immediately set about exploring his surroundings. The room could only be described as palatial. It was decorated in cream and gold and contained a reception room, a bedroom with a larger bed than Jussi had ever seen, and a bathroom. The centrepiece of which was an enormous jacuzzi bath.

Jussi removed his laptop and put down his bag. Before sitting down to work, he couldn't resist pouring himself a vodka and tonic from the impressive range of bottles lined up in the complimentary chilled bar. He also enjoyed a few chocolates from the box set out on the small table by the sofa.

After spending an hour updating a couple of files and dealing with emails, he settled back with a second drink and put his feet up for a while.

He considered his current situation. Instead of taking a leading role in Russia, in what was now an international investigation, he was to be rewarded and returned to Finland. No doubt, he would still be involved from a distance; however, he would probably receive another case or two. Maybe, this time it would just be someone stealing mobile phones?

Jussi's aspirations had been growing, and he could now see

himself as a successful detective; as such, he was reluctant to see his role diminish.

Suddenly, he looked at his watch - it was almost time to go, so he quickly freshened up in the bathroom, changed his shirt and donned a smart black suit. Suitably attired for a formal night out at the ballet, he left his room to meet Janis downstairs.

He found Janis already in the reception area, reading a newspaper, who looked up at his arrival. He was also decked out in a dark suit; actually, he was dressed entirely in black.

"Hi Jussi, feeling refreshed? Did you sample the complimentary bar?"

Jussi nodded, "Oh yes and very good it was too. I tested a couple of the vodkas and I may try a vintage cognac later."

"Count on it," replied Janis. "My police duties don't usually include nights like this."

They walked outside where a car was waiting for them: a large black saloon that whisked them away to the restaurant. Their driver, who introduced himself simply as 'Alex', gave them a running commentary of some of the sights they passed.

Jussi marvelled at the Winter Palace and made a mental note to revisit Saint Petersburg sometime, to enjoy it properly. He could invite Selma. Then, he suddenly remembered. He had utterly forgotten about Selma and realized he didn't have her number either, as his phone had been stolen.

"Damn," he said under his breath.

"You okay?" asked Janis with concern.

"Yeh, I'm fine. I just remembered something. Nothing important, though."

The car drew up to the restaurant. It was a fine establishment and decidedly upscale, similar to the hotel in which they were staying.

"Wow," Janis exclaimed. I'm happy we're not paying this bill."

They gave their names at the door and were welcomed like royalty.

"Please order whatever you wish. It's all taken care of," the Maître d' informed.

The restaurant was busy and seemed full of wealthy Russians, with a particular bias towards younger women. Jussi commented that he could smell the money in the room as everything looked so expensive. The two detectives thoroughly enjoyed their dinner. While not wanting to abuse the hospitality, they did make the most of delicious caviar, excellent steak and a fine pavlova. They also accepted the wine tasting menu and drank a selection of perfect wines to match each course.

They sat back and relaxed at the end of dinner with large cognacs in hand, clinking their glasses at their good fortune.

Then, it was onto the opera. The car was waiting for them across the road, and Alex drove them the short distance to the Maryanski Teat, where the performance was to be held. The building was eye-wateringly beautiful, situated adjacent to the River Neva.

Jussi and Janis made their way inside. After collecting the pre-booked tickets at the box office, they settled down to watch the opera. The show was the 'Queen of Spades' and was a magnificent spectacle to behold.

During the performance, Jussi found his mind wandering back to Selma again and how much she might enjoy coming to something like this. He resolved to track down her phone number or, at the very least, visit her apartment when he returned.

It was a long performance, and both the detectives were weary at the end but nonetheless appreciative. They made their way out to the waiting car, and after a few words, Alex turned the car towards their hotel.

They were both almost asleep in the car on arrival, so bade each other goodnight and left for their rooms.

Jussi opened the door to his hotel room and decided he would take that cognac before bed. He opened the double doors of the small balcony and breathed deeply.

The night of Saint Petersburg was stretched out in front of him. He looked around the room, thinking about his evening, shaking his head at the thought of the life some people must enjoy.

He remembered Selma again. A memory had just entered his mind: he had made a booking for the kayaks and had entered both their phone numbers in the booking so they would both receive any messages about it. It was one of those thoughts that his subconscious had been dealing with for a few hours now, but it had only just arrived in his conscious mind for attention. He immediately went to open his laptop and switched it on - nothing happened.

"Damn, I left it on," he muttered to himself.

He remembered he had packed light and hadn't packed a charger, so he picked up his laptop and headed downstairs to reception.

Jussi was impressed to discover the reception had a wide range of charging cables and adapters, and thanked them profusely for having his type available. He sat down on one of the sofas in the lobby and powered up his device.

After a few minutes of searching, he found Selma's number. It was too late to call now, and he had left his phone in the room anyway; therefore, he decided to send a message via his laptop. He composed a note explaining he had lost his phone, was in Saint Petersburg and hoped to see her on his return to Helsinki. With his mission accomplished, he walked up to his room to charge his laptop overnight and get some sleep.

As he approached the room, he noticed the door was slightly ajar. Had he left it like that in his haste? Or was someone else in there?

Jussi carefully opened the door and looked in through the gap. He could see someone's back as they searched his bag. Jussi opened the door carefully. The man seemed to be fully occupied. Sensing danger, though, the man suddenly turned around.

By instinct, Jussi immediately slammed the laptop into his face, sending him flying onto the floor. Then, he glimpsed a second man coming at him from the bathroom. He decided the best course of action was to get out of there and, seeing the man reaching for something that he could only presume was a gun, he ran for the door and slammed it shut behind him.

Jussi sprinted down the corridor, trying to remember Janis's room number. It was on the same floor, but he couldn't recall which one. Reaching what he thought might be it, he knocked on the door, but there was no answer. Then he moved along to his second choice and knocked on that door. He tried the handle, and it opened.

Inside, in a similar room to his own, he was shocked to find a body lying face down on the carpet, with blood on its back. He knelt, rolled the body over and found Janis's face looking up at him. He was dead. Jussi rose and shook his head in disbelief. He had seen a body before, but never this close. Neither had he seen one with whom he had just spent the day.

Suddenly, a combination of adrenalin and training kicked in, and he ran to the door, closing it quietly and locking it.

He checked Janis's belongings for anything that may be useful. There was nothing - everything had been taken. Jussi's mind was racing now. He heard the door handle and saw it move downwards, but he had already locked it. He made his decision: right now, he had to get out of the hotel. On checking the balcony, he found it was too high up. He saw a door leading off somewhere else and dashed through it. It was a small kitchenette with a back door, which he opened and saw that it lead down a spiral staircase.

"Fire exit," he breathed.

He went through it and quietly closed the door behind him. He ran and jumped down each of the landings. He was on the 6th floor, so it wouldn't take long to reach the bottom.

When he got to the stairwell, he stopped and listened. He couldn't hear anything. He cast a glance towards two doors at opposite ends of the landing. One probably led into the hotel and the other towards an external exit. He considered his options: he could walk straight into a bullet if they knew about the fire exit, but one of the doors must open to the outside. He swiftly made his choice and opened it.

Outside was a small alley with various buildings' fire exits leading into an area with trash bins. One end was closed by a large iron gate, so selecting the only available way forward, he left the door ajar behind him, just in case, it might be his only escape. Then, he weaved his way through the alley, using the bins as cover. At the end of it, he saw the main road and assumed he must be at the rear of the hotel.

After a brief look around, he chose a direction and walked quickly away. He crossed the road as soon as possible and continued walking briskly away from the hotel. He saw some shops and made his way towards them.

It was drizzling now, so he stepped into a men's clothing store and bought a tan coloured raincoat and black umbrella. Now he had a disguise. After a cursory glance behind him, Jussi walked away into the night.

THE FUGITIVE

Gregor sat down in his private office chair and opened his laptop. He booted it up, clicked the virtual meeting link, and Natalya's face appeared on the screen.

"Dobry Vecher, Natalja. Do you have any news?" he asked.

"We have eliminated the Latvian policeman in Saint Petersburg; however, we're still searching for the Finnish one."

"Well, that's something at least. Please keep me informed. We should sever the Finnish connection as soon as possible. What about Edgars?"

"He contacted us this afternoon, and we'll meet him at the prearranged meeting point tomorrow morning. I have enough men available to conclude his involvement."

"Excellent, I knew that you would clear this mess up for me. If you need more of the team in Saint Petersburg to find this Jussi, let me know. I would like to see the end of this within 24 hours. Then, you can arrange a new office with a new company name, and we can start rebuilding again."

"Da. That will be done. It'll be a simple job to recommence operations in Latvia again. We can then begin planning our way forward into Finland once more."

"Oh yes, about that. I've already decided to purchase some property there. It will be easier if we own an office than have any external involvement. I'll deal with that. Just finish what we need to do, Natalja."

◆ ◆ ◆

Selma sat on her bed with her legs crossed, wearing pyjamas. She had opened her laptop intending to work on her open university course but couldn't concentrate.

After receiving Jussi's message, and against her better judgment, she replied that she was looking forward to seeing him again sometime. She had added 'sometime' so as not to look too keen to see him. In reality, Selma was still angry with him and didn't completely buy his excuses, but she had decided to give him a chance. There was something different about Jussi. She had grown very fond of him in the short time they had been seeing each other.

She didn't receive a reply to her text but wasn't surprised, as it was late and she knew that it was one hour later in Saint Petersburg, so he was probably asleep. She logged off and closed the laptop - time to sleep, herself. She would probably hear from him in the morning.

◆ ◆ ◆

By coincidence, Jussi was thinking of Selma at that very moment.

He had checked into a small hotel in a less salubrious part of town and was sat in his locked room, pondering his next steps. He had lost his temporary mobile phone and left his probably broken laptop in his hotel room. He had no way of contacting Selma right now as he didn't remember her number. Jussi would have given anything to have had her here with him. He cursed himself for being too busy to contact her before losing his phone. He would try to make things right when he returned to Helsinki.

conscious, sitting among the Russian clientele, so he decided to look out of the window, hoping the television in the corner wouldn't be switched on.

After ten minutes, the burger arrived, and the old man looked at his watch, gesturing to Jussi that they would be closing at midnight, in twenty minutes. Jussi nodded his head and ate the burger like a man who didn't know where his next meal was coming from. Some blue lights passed the bar, and he stiffened, but thankfully, they turned the corner and disappeared.

He waited until the last moment and left the bar when everyone else had gone, wandering slowly back to the hotel, checking the surrounding area as he did so. He turned a corner and saw blue lights

Should I walk over to them? he asked himself.

Something made him cross the road, and he returned to the shadows of a small street.

"How did I get myself into this?" Jussi whispered to himself as he walked away from the hotel.

Luckily, he hadn't left anything in his room except his new umbrella. Everything else that he possessed was on his back at that moment, and he had his wallet in his jacket. He patted his pocket for reassurance every so often, as it was now probably his only lifeline.

He continued onwards, without knowing the direction and suddenly became aware of a car moving slowly behind him. He crossed the road and noted the vehicle following his route.

This doesn't look good, he decided.

He turned a corner once more and ran. The car sped up, and he continued to run, checking everywhere for somewhere that might be open. There was no shelter anywhere. Suddenly, another car appeared in front of him, and the one behind him closed in. There was nowhere to go, so he stopped and waited for what might happen.

"Jussi Alonen?" a voice asked in a heavy Russian accent.

He said nothing in reply.

"Please get in the car. You have nowhere to go here."

Jussi looked around and saw two men get out of the car in front. Having no choice, he walked towards the vehicle, and a door was opened for him to get in. The two men sat on either side of him, and both cars drove away.

Shortly afterwards, one of the men pulled out a hood and placed it over Jussi's head. He could no longer see what was happening and felt some covers placed over his ears. Now, all he could do was to wait and hope.

It was another half an hour before he felt the car come to a halt, and the hood and earphones were removed. Jussi had lost track of time but knew it was early in the morning. He looked around as he was marched toward a log cabin and taken inside. He was relieved to see that he was not being mistreated, at least not yet anyway. The place looked like a hunting lodge, and inside was decorated with leather chairs and animal trophies lined the walls.

He was surprised to be offered coffee and a seat on entering, and he accepted both. He had decided that there was little chance of escape as three men were in the room with him and probably more outside. Even with his hands untied, he probably wouldn't even get as far as the door. So, he waited and considered his options while watching the clock on the wall ahead, which now read 1.40 am.

At about 2.00 am, the door opened and in walked a man with an unmistakable air of authority. Another followed him. Both wore black leather jackets and jeans. The first man wore a flat cap, and Jussi deduced him to be the leader.

"Hello, Jussi. Well, it's nice to meet you at last. So, you're the one that has been digging into my organisation, causing havoc everywhere."

Jussi sat quietly and listened.

"I've researched you, and it seems you are quite a young hero? Although, you have made a few mistakes and ruffled a few feathers. Now, you're ruffling mine, and I need to do something about it."

"Who are you?" asked Jussi.

"My name is Gregor, and I'm the leader of the organisation you've been so interested in. So, Jussi, why have you been so interested in the Vipers?"

"Well, let's begin with murder, kidnapping, theft, smuggling and criminal damage. I am sure we could go on with the list."

"Are you accusing me of these things? Jussi, these things happen every day, in every country of the world. I have no interest in such matters. I deal in money. Some of my associates may do some of these things, but not me."

Jussi studied him and asked, "Why am I being kept here? I have no influence here in Russia. They were going to send me back to Finland. Also, why kill Janis?"

"I told you. I don't do things like that," Gregor replied. "You will have to speak to the people concerned. As to why you are being held here? I knew you would be sent back to Finland, but you are just too tenacious Jussi. I can't have you damaging my organisation more than you have done already. Now, I need to decide what to do with you?"

"The Latvian operation has been dismantled now, so If you release me, you won't see me again. I have no interest in what if you do here. Just let me go."

"I'm afraid that's impossible. We're already re-building our Latvian operation and then we will continue in Helsinki. You see, I want Helsinki to be our platform to enter the other Nordic countries. We have a big business opportunity, and you have become a barrier that we need to remove. It's a pity because I could really use someone like you. What do you think Jussi? Would you like to earn some big money and help us to grow our business in Finland?"

"You know the answer to that question, Gregor. I'm a police officer."

"I thought so. It's a shame because now I will have to hand you over to my associates, and I'm unsure what they will do? Well, it was nice meeting you. Goodbye, Jussi."

Gregor walked out of the room before Jussi could think what to say. One of the men made a phone call and nodded whilst talking in Russian. Jussi couldn't pick out any of the conversations apart from the fact that the man was receiving instructions. They took the coffee cup away from Jussi and bound his hands to the chair. The men left the cabin and went outside.

Jussi struggled with the cable ties locking his hands together, but it was no use. He looked around the room for anything that might help him. He heard the cars drive away, and managed to half-stand with the chair and shuffle his way over to the window. All of the vehicles were gone.

"What the hell is happening now?" Jussi breathed.

It was time to do something, and he tried to smash the chair against the wall. He did this, and the struts came away effortlessly. He freed his hands from the chair and headed to the kitchen area. He found a rack of knives and managed to remove one and cut his hands free. He took the knife with him and checked around the cabin. There was little more of use, but he took matches from the fireplace and a blanket from one of the chairs.

He made for the back door, which was locked. He looked around and noticed a briefcase, which he opened and checked the contents within. He rifled through the papers and found some letters and receipts with his name on them. He also found photographs of boats.

"What the?"

The more Jussi looked, the more he decided he was being set up. Next, he heard police sirens in the distance. It didn't take long for Jussi to realize they were coming for him, and they had set him up. What better way than just killing him than implicating him in something and moving the suspicion away from the Russians. That's why it hadn't been difficult for him to escape. Things were more complicated than he had time for, but the briefcase was definitely coming with him. He slammed it shut and used it to smash the back window. He managed to break its lock and then used a knife to lever the window open. Then he jumped through it, into the dark. As he did so, he saw blue lights flashing and instinctively ran. He didn't know how to fix everything right now and had to get to a safe place to think of a plan. Now, though, he needed to run again.

Jussi set off through the woods as best he could. He ran painfully into a branch and was aware of voices far behind him. He kept running as fast as he could into the pitch darkness.

Finally, he made it to a road. He saw headlights and flagged down an old car that slowed to a halt. The driver spoke some broken English.

"Yes, I give you lift. Come!" the driver said. Then he asked, "Do you like buy special coin?"

On the way, Jussi found himself buying an old coin in

exchange for the ride, but didn't resent it at all. He was being taken away from danger and back towards the relative safety of Saint Petersburg.

Several police cars swept by on the way, presumably for his benefit. He wondered if the man knew they were coming for him.

"Where I take you?" the old man asked in broken English.

"I don't know, somewhere in the centre maybe?" Jussi replied.

"You nowhere go?"

"No," said Jussi. "Actually, I haven't," he answered, considering his next move.

"Then, this night, you come home me!" the older man stated.

Jussi was exhausted, sweating and could feel the blood trickling down his face from where a branch had scratched it. This was the best offer on the table, so he accepted it gratefully.

Ten minutes later, they arrived at a group of tall, forbidding Soviet-era apartments, and the older man drove the car into a roughly-made carpark nearby. The man, who introduced himself as Fyodor, slowly led him up steps to a higher floor and showed him into his apartment.

"First, vodka! Then sleep," he told Jussi, who nodded with a smile.

Fyodor opened the fridge and fixed two large glasses of vodka, handing one to Jussi.

"Za Droozhboo," he announced, as they clinked glasses.

Jussi had no idea what it meant but toasted regardless. Of course, the man didn't speak Finnish, and without much English either, it was a challenging conversation. However, with the aid of the vodka, they somehow made it work. Jussi asked if he had a phone, but he didn't.

At around 4 am, covered by an old blanket, Jussi finally fell asleep on the sofa.

DIPLOMATIC RELATIONS

Tapio drummed on the edge of his desk with his pen. He was worried. He'd been told that Jussi would arrive at Vantaa airport in the morning, and he hadn't. In fact, he hadn't even boarded the flight. He'd also learned from the office in Riga, that Janis hadn't returned either.

He took his cup of coffee and headed towards the conference table for the regular morning case update. Once seated, he asked if he could begin the meeting and started with the news, or rather lack of it, concerning Jussi.

During the meeting, Tapio's phone rang. He noted that it was a Latvian number, so he excused himself to take the call. It was alarming news. The Russian Police had communicated that Janis had been found dead in his hotel room. In addition, Jussi had disappeared and was a suspect in the murder case. The room erupted with voices as the team exchanged heated views. The Detective Inspector stood up and waved his arms for everyone to calm down.

"Okay, relax, everyone," Pekka directed. "How they can suspect Jussi of anything is ridiculous, but the fact that he has disappeared is even more concerning. For all we know, he could be in trouble? Or wounded? Or worse? I want you to investigate how? when? and why this could have happened? to see if you can think of anything that might help. I'm going upstairs, as we'll need some help from the Government."

With that, Pekka headed towards the lift.

❖ ❖ ❖

Jussi awoke and checked his watch - it was dead and out of battery, so he leaned over to view a clock that sat on the mantlepiece. It was 9.35 am, and he hadn't expected to sleep this late.

Perhaps the vodka knocked me out, he thought, feeling a headache coming on.

There was no sign of the older man, but a pot of coffee and savoury pastries were on the table, so Jussi sat down and ate breakfast.

When he'd finished, he checked the other rooms just in case Fyodor was still in the apartment, but he was nowhere to be found. Jussi had a wash, gathered his few possessions and left some euros on the table. Then, he left the apartment, taking care to lock it on his way out. He felt extremely grateful to the stranger who had rescued him and resolved to thank him properly someday.

It was drizzling with rain as he walked through the grey, forbidding apartment blocks, but he was pleased to come across a taxi rank after a few minutes. He waved at one of them, and shortly afterwards, they were slowly meandering through the heavy Saint Petersburg morning traffic. He asked the driver to take him to the Finnish Consulate, and they arrived at the gate within an hour. Jussi paid the driver, talked to the guard at the gate, and was escorted to the building. Jussi heaved a long sigh of relief as he entered Finnish territory.

❖ ❖ ❖

In Helsinki, the team sat around the conference table were discussing the situation in Riga when the Inspector burst into the room.

"There's some news," he exclaimed. "Jussi has just walked into the Finnish Consulate in Saint Petersburg. Tapio, I need the whole file. Get everything together and come with me. We're going to meet with our Minister of Foreign Affairs."

◆ ◆ ◆

Jussi poured himself another coffee and stood up, pacing the room. After a debriefing, he had been told that the officials in Finland would do all they could to extract him as soon as possible. However, at this point, he would have to stay inside the Consulate for as long as necessary. He had been racking his brains about how they could put an end to Gregor's plan. If he couldn't convince the Russian authorities of his innocence and Gregor's involvement, everything would continue as Gregor had told him. There would be no way of getting at the gang leader outside Russia, and Jussi couldn't walk out of the Consulate for fear of being arrested. Things had become very complicated.

One of the consulate officers walked into the room and introduced himself. He was the third person Jussi had met here so far, and he couldn't help wondering if the Consulate staff had ever experienced such a complex situation before.

"Right. Progress," the man announced. "We've managed to reach your inspector, and he will meet with the Finnish Foreign Ministry this afternoon. Hopefully, they will get an appointment with the Russian Embassy in Helsinki today or tomorrow, and negotiations will begin for your safe passage home to Finland."

Jussi heaved a sigh of relief and sank further into the chair. This plan sounded hopeful.

"Let's not forget about the Vipers or whoever they are?" Jussi commented. "I don't doubt that I have a target on my head now."

"Well, I assume that after conversations have taken place between our government and the Russians, we will invite them to interview you here, where we know you are safe. Then, we can reach an agreement to proceed with your extradition. I'm sure they'll get you to the airport safely. They won't want to upset diplomatic relations further, especially as the man killed in the hotel room wasn't Russian either, whoever he was."

Jussi flashed him a warning glance and said, "Janis was a friend."

"Sorry," the man coughed. "Anyway, we can move forward. Until then, please try and relax. Use this room as your own and if you need anything, just let me know. We'll send out for some clothes and other things you will need."

"May I use a computer and a phone, please?" Jussi asked.

The man disappeared for a moment and returned with a laptop.

"Here you are. It's a spare one; I'll log it in for you. For the phone, just dial 9 for an outside line."

A few minutes later, Jussi punched Selma's number into the phone.

"Hello," a familiar voice answered.

"Selma. It's Jussi. So nice to hear your voice. Have I got some news to tell you?"

❖ ❖ ❖

The interview with the Russian police was arranged for the following morning. Jussi had the use of a guest room within the consulate and had been advised not to leave the premises for any reason. He was happy to abide by this direction and spent the evening preparing his case.

Several calls took place between the task force members, mainly with Tapio. Jussi was relieved to have Tapio supporting him; he felt that he had his back.

Jussi followed up his previous call with Selma with another. His initial contact had been received in quite a cool manner, and she had not been as desperate to speak to him as he had hoped. However, once Jussi had explained the whole story of the events over the past week, Selma was amazed and understood everything. A few things that Jussi didn't mention to Selma were probably better forgotten. Anyway, he had already cursed himself for almost messing up his potential relationship with Selma on several occasions and was determined to regain her trust. To this end, he had asked her to dinner on his return, and she had agreed. That was enough at this point.

The Russian police had already spent some time at the hotel's crime scene, and Jussi's DNA was found all over it. The gun had been found in his bag, in his room, but without any fingerprints. Jussi would need a solid case to explain the situation. His argument would be based on the whole story as there was no point in keeping anything back now. Additional evidence would also be presented; namely, the investigation found that Janis had called somewhere in Latvia, just as he was interrupted by the shots. At that same time, Jussi had been observed in the lobby by the reception staff.

There was also no motive for the murder, especially given the final evening they had shared. There was an additional point in Jussi's favour: although a case was being compiled against him, the investigating officer wasn't convinced of Jussi's guilt. He had, in fact, already formed an opinion that this was all the work of organised crime.

◆ ◆ ◆

Jussi awoke early the following day. He'd been so tired that he'd fallen asleep shortly after 9 pm, and felt much better after more than nine hours' sleep. He made his way down to the communal kitchen, fixed himself some cereal and put coffee on the stove. He was probably the only person in the building that used the old-fashioned expresso maker, but after trying it the day before, he loved the strength of the coffee it delivered and resolved to buy one for his own apartment.

After breakfast, he brought the laptop and anything on paper down to his borrowed office. He spent the next hours going through everything again. The meeting was approaching, and Erkki Lehtinen, the consulate lawyer, joined him. They spent the next hour and a half going through their case and getting ready. After this preparation, they were satisfied they had prepared adequately.

The appointed time came, and the Russian delegation arrived: two men and a woman. They introduced each other formally, one by one. One was the investigating officer, Anatoly Lebedev, and the second was his Assistant, Vasily Kuznestov. The third was a representative from the Russian Interior Ministry, Zoya Smirnov. On the Finnish side was Jussi, accompanied by Erkki, the lawyer, and a young secretary, named Herta.

The three Finns sat along one side of the table. The Russian contingent did the same and spent some time removing various folders and files, together with their laptops. Erkki acted as Host and ensured that everyone had coffee or tea, plus cold bottles of water. Once this was done and notepads and pens were set out on the table ready, they began.

It was a straightforward meeting, and Jussi was pleasantly

surprised that Anatoly was immediately on his side. Once the evidence was pieced together, the scenario became so unlikely that Anatoly changed the agenda of the meeting entirely and started pressing for more information about Gregor. He revealed they already had a portfolio of evidence against him, but it was not enough to secure a conviction. He explained that when they located any witnesses, they had a way of mysteriously changing their story or even disappearing altogether.

The meeting lasted most of the day and only broke for a short lunch of sandwiches and a couple of short coffee breaks.
When the meeting was over, Anatoly shook Jussi's hand and arranged another meeting for the following day to formulate a plan to move against Gregor. He requested if Jussi would remain in Russia for a few days or at least as much time as was necessary to prepare the arrest warrant. Jussi trusted Anatoly and was only too happy to help.

After the meeting, Jussi called Selma again. He didn't want to make the same mistake and slip off her radar again. This time she was pleased to hear from him. Her feelings had changed for the better - perhaps she had forgiven at least some of his behaviour?

DESPERATE MEASURES

Natalja surveyed her new office with satisfaction. It would be the perfect place to commence operations in Riga. She was secretly quite happy about recent events because this had placed Latvia and potentially the whole Baltic region directly under her command. Now it was just a matter of organization. She had already regrouped the men that had worked for Edgars and brought them firmly under her control. She had also appointed one of them to refurbish the office under her direction. The space was receiving her very particular design preferences.

She had the rest of the men on the road, talking with suppliers, buyers and others with whom there was some kind of a business relationship. Continuity was the priority before considering expansion.

The next phase of the operation would be to eradicate the influence of Edgars. He may still be in contact with some of his men, and whilst he was alive, there would be no permanent closure and rebirth of the business. She already had feelers out in various directions, including the police, a member of which had contacted her and offered to provide the necessary information as soon as it was available. However, today, Edgars was still at large and no doubt hiding somewhere until it was safe to leave the country. The sooner she tracked him down, the better. Natalja was ambitious, and when properly motivated, she was a force to be reckoned with.

◆ ◆ ◆

Since the police operation, Edgars had been at the hideout, but escaped as soon as the search had subsided. He knew dogs would be brought in sooner or later, and so under cover of night, they used an inflatable dinghy to slip away, rowing slowly down the coast until they were far enough from the base to reach the road safely. Then, it had been a simple matter of flagging down a vehicle and getting a lift towards Ventspils.

They turned off the road in case of roadblocks, found a small unoccupied cabin in the trees, and Edgars' bodyguard disposed of the car's driver. They sat in the log cabin while Edgars used the smartphone from the unfortunate driver to search the web for potential escape routes.

In the end, they decided to remain at the cabin for a couple of days and then make their way to a friendly supply ship that often helped Edgars with shipping orders. They would be able to get a bunk to Germany, and from there, with the aid of Edgars' bank accounts, they planned to hide and recover some of what had been lost. Edgars wasn't going to take the chance of calling any associates at this stage; he decided to do that after he was safe himself.

Edgars was an intelligent man, but he had misjudged how advanced the Latvian authorities were in tracing mobile phones. As soon as the victim was reported missing from the Ventspils road, the Latvian police began to trace his mobile phone and alerted OMEGA. Unbeknown to Edgars, while he was enjoying a bottle of red wine they found in a cupboard, paramilitary officers encircled the cabin.

The order was given, and OMEGA sprang into action. They rammed the cabin door and aimed their guns. The two fugitives immediately grabbed their weapons and dived into the hallway, firing. However, the OMEGA squad shot back with unforgiving accuracy, and both shooters fell where they stood, without a single officer receiving injuries.

◆ ◆ ◆

When Natalja heard from her police source that the previous incumbent of the Latvian business had been gunned down, she took a bottle of vodka from her office fridge and toasted herself. The Latvian police had done the job for her. Now she could focus upon the business and let the old empire die with Edgars. She couldn't wait to call Gregor and tell him the news that Latvia was back in business once again, under her direction.

"Da?" Gregor answered his phone with his customary greeting.

Then, he laughed out loud. Some of Gregor's associates were in the meeting room and were unused to hearing him laugh where business was concerned. They looked at each other curiously. After the call, Gregor confidently announced that Latvia was back in business, and he had chosen the right person for the job.

Meanwhile, the Russian Police were as effective in their ability to trace mobile communications as their Latvian counterparts. Anatoly was extremely interested in the recording and transcript he received later that day. He took pleasure in calling Jussi and informing him that they had just come across damning evidence to prove Gregor was involved in criminal operations in Latvia.

He invited Jussi to the station and sent an armed escort to bring him, just in case. By this time, both Jussi and the Finnish police department were comfortable about him leaving the consulate, provided he had adequate protection.

At this stage, the Pan-European task force was regularly

cooperating, and the Russian contingent had been integrated within the group. It was within everyone's interests that Russia curtailed the criminal organisation's activities to prevent its expansion into Europe.

As Jussi had been involved with almost everything, his opinion was sought in the development of a plan. They discussed various strategies, but when it all came down to it, they had enough evidence to move on the Vipers and proposed to do so before the organisation could recover and get back in business.

Twenty-four hours of discussion later, everyone had agreed to move forward in the same direction: it was time to go after the head of the snake, Gregor Ivanov.

FRONTAL ASSAULT

It was just after 4.30 am, and the day had started to break. It had been a short, cold night, and the sun's warmth was only just beginning to cut through the chill. A haze had developed as the warm air mixed with cold and dissipated over the ground.

The assault team assembled two kilometres away at a road junction where several vehicles lined up in a row. The bulk of the group was from OMON, the Russian Special Purpose Police Team, and Anatoly was leading what had now evolved into a full-scale assault plan. The local Commander of OMON and the Area Police Chief stood discussing final details, as Jussi looked on as an observer. Anatoly had requested that he be available to provide any valuable insights into the organisation and identify Gregor on the ground should he try and escape.

In total, there were forty men, most of them heavily armed, spread throughout six vehicles, including two troop carriers. The house and grounds were substantial, and in addition to the direct assault force, Anatoly wanted men around the perimeter. Jussi thought it looked like a war zone, but the Russians knew Gregor's type, and they preferred to go in heavy rather than risk a prolonged gunfight.

Suddenly, everyone was ready, and it was time to go. The convoy vehicles accelerated, with OMON in the lead. They drove closely together at speed, and Jussi wondered how they didn't crash into each other. Anatoly explained that it was standard procedure in these situations to prevent any vehicle from interrupting the convoy.

They approached the large mansion, and as they did so, the night guards on the gate sounded an alarm and dived for cover. The troop carrier in the lead crashed straight through the gates, and half the vehicles followed. The other half either stopped fifty metres from the entrance or swerved to each side of the perimeter.

The gunfire started almost immediately. The guards at the gate had no idea who was attacking them and instinctively started firing from the gatehouse. Anatoly's car stopped, together with some of the police and OMON vehicles, side by side, forming an effective barrier, from which they swiftly returned retaliatory shots.

Meanwhile, two other OMON vehicles stopped near the house, and the squad disembarked. One of the officers jumped into the gun turret and covered the house with a powerful machine gun while the remainder of the team dropped to the ground, ready to target any signs of life.

Despite the gunfire at the gatehouse, there was no activity. The commander waited for two minutes and waved some of the team forward in a flanking movement towards the wall. They ran over to it, with the other half of the team ready to open fire.

By this time, the security guards at the gate had realized that it was the police and they were considerably out-gunned, so the firing stopped as they surrendered.

Back at the house, the advance team moved closer to the main building. More men ran to the opposite side of the mansion and edged closer to the grand doorway, edging up against the wall.

It looked like a straightforward entry, and one of the men edged forward with a battering ram, protected by another officer, holding a large shield. When they reached the door, they waited for the signal, then rammed into it.

The size of the explosion which followed shocked everyone. The door blew away, and pieces of masonry, metal and wood flew in all directions. The officers at the door were blown back onto the driveway, and others, preparing to enter, fell to the ground. Smoke encircled the whole area. There were shouts everywhere, and the officers were ordered to hold their ground, lest there be more potential bombs or booby traps.

When the smoke subsided, the size of the devastation was visible. A huge, gaping hole had replaced the whole entrance. Officers dragged themselves to a firing position, while medics ran to the wounded, removing the severely injured.

Everyone stood ready while the commander called headquarters for bomb disposal support. Ambulances began to arrive, and the assault was momentarily halted.

While all this was going on, Gregor sat in his safe room office, pondering his next move. He had distributed his men throughout the house, but didn't expect them to be able to hold out for too long against the strength of OMON. However, he was safe for now, as it would take some time for them to find the room and a construction team to create access. On balance, though, he decided it was time to move. There would only be more OMON or police outside as time went on, and it was safer to try and escape now rather than be boxed in later.

He walked over to his safe, opened it and removed some documents and valuables. He placed them in his briefcase, together with the laptop from his desk, a handgun, and an ammunition box. Next, he lifted the carpet, revealing a trapdoor that he opened. He dropped into the space and made his way downwards. There was a thick steel door that protected his office from underground, which he opened, revealing another tunnel. When Gregor had first moved into the house, the escape tunnel had been one of his most significant investments. Now, it had paid off.

Gregor started to move down the narrow passage on all fours; wooden panels lined the sides, protecting it from the surrounding earth. It took seven minutes for him to make his way through the tunnel to a trapdoor at the other side. There was another interior steel door ahead that he opened with a firm tug. A ladder led upwards, and he climbed up, opening a door at the top. It didn't move for a moment, so he pushed forcefully. It gave way and spread into what was basically a metal box. He stepped inside and closed the door. From the exterior, the metal hut was disguised as an electrical utility maintenance unit and was easily ignored.

Gregor orientated himself for a moment and switched on a small light. A yellow lamp illuminated the space, which had a door at one end. Half of it was taken up by a motorcycle. Gregor opened a small chest in the corner containing an overall and helmet and moved the bike forwards to the door. He planned that his men would defend the house for as long as possible, providing him with enough time to escape. It would be hours before they got into the safe room and discovered he had already fled.

Gregor put on the overall, pulled the helmet down in front of his face and unbolted the door. Easing the motorcycle through, he mounted it and switched on the ignition. It roared into life, and he set off immediately, away from his beloved mansion. It was unlikely he would ever see the house again; however, there would be other houses in the future. He roared off into the distance and headed for the countryside.

◆ ◆ ◆

As soon as the security guards at the entrance had given up and surrendered, Jussi followed Anatoly through the gate. OMON threw the guards onto the ground and handcuffed them.

Some of the team advanced along the driveway towards the house on foot, leaving the remaining officers with the vehicles at the entrance, lest anyone should try and escape.

Jussi ran up the gravel drive and had a clear view of the doorway explosion when it happened. Nobody had expected it. Everyone stopped running and fell to their knees with guns drawn, however, the gunfire that he envisioned to follow never came. As the smoke billowed out, they continued to run and arrived at the parked OMON vehicles. The commander and Anatoly had a brief conversation and decided there was nothing to gain by waiting and moved in.

As they entered the house, the officers moving to the right found nothing. However, those on the left encountered heavy resistance. A gun battle ensued, with fierce fighting on both sides; the noise was deafening.

After twenty minutes, more OMON and police moved in, the firepower increased, and shots found their way to wound the remaining guards; resistance was soon overpowered.

It took some time before they discovered the safe room behind one of the wooden panels. It didn't take long for them to learn that it was virtually impregnable. They brought in experts, and work commenced slowly. Jussi observed the task and decided it would take days at this rate.

"Do you think he's in there?" Jussi asked.

"I don't think so. I think we lost him somewhere in the chaos. There would be no point in staying in there. Unless, of course, he has some damn good vodka!" Anatoly replied.

"Do you know where he might have gone?" asked Jussi, looking out of the large window.

"I was about to ask you the same question," Anatoly answered. "We know he was in the house, don't we? And the land is too exposed for him to have got away across it. No cars were taken, but the explosion and the gunfire provided time for something."

"Could there be an escape tunnel?"

Anatoly regarded Jussi thoughtfully.

"You could be right. It sounds a little far-fetched, but you could still be correct. It'll take a long time to gain access to the safe room, so in the meantime, let's check the perimeter."

The detectives walked out of the house, back towards the gate and began inspecting the outside walls. It wasn't long before they found the small metal hut and gained entry.

"I can't believe it," commented Anatoly looking around. "Judging by the equipment here, he had a motorcycle, and who knows what else?"

Jussi lifted the trapdoor and peered inside.

"Here."

Anatoly removed a torch, hanging conveniently on the wall and handed it to Jussi. He jumped inside, and Anatoly spoke into his radio to update the team, following Jussi down the tunnel.

After some minutes of shuffling along, they found the metal ladder at the other side, opened the steel door and emerged through the trapdoor. They stood up and looked around the office, shaking their heads in disbelief.

"So, he was prepared that he might need to do this one day. That's some organisation," Anatoly commented in disbelief.

Jussi rifled through the drawers in the desk. He was aware that this wasn't protocol, but he needed to find a piece of evidence that might pinpoint the whereabouts of Gregor quickly. Anatoly joined him at the desk.

With no success, Jussi scanned the shelves and read some of the boxes.

"This looks like the accounts of the business. I'm sure there's plenty of useful stuff here," Jussi remarked as they continued searching.

Jussi found a file marked property and skimmed through a selection of houses and commercial property. He was surprised to come across one in Helsinki. Interested, he read through the details.

"This place is in Helsinki. He already has a place in Finland; it's an office block."

"His Finnish HQ maybe," commented Anatoly.

Jussi took a photograph with his phone, returning it to his pocket.

"Let's get all of this catalogued now," Anatoly directed as he unlocked the door using a button on the keypad.

He welcomed the waiting officers to assist. Jussi and Anatoly subsequently left the team, who would begin cataloguing and photographing the room's contents.

As Jussi walked through the house, he was impressed by the size of the Russian operation, engaged in the task in hand, beginning to break down the organisation of the infamous Vipers.

◆ ◆ ◆

It had been a long day, and Jussi was ready to relax. Now Gregor was on the run, it seemed safe to return to a hotel; however, Anatoly had still advised against it. Therefore, he was back at the Consulate once more. As an added precaution, paramilitary police guards now stood outside the building.

Later in the evening, Jussi poured himself a large gin and tonic and stretched out on an easy chair in the lounge. It'd been hard to process the chain of events over the past weeks. The last case he had been involved in had been surreal, but this one was nothing short of incredible.

♦ ♦ ♦

The next day passed with little activity. Jussi remained at the Consulate and spent most of the day with his head in his laptop. There was no communication from Anatoly, and aside from a check-in meeting with the team in Helsinki, everything seemed to have gone quiet. With the disappearance of Gregor, there was little to do here now.

Later in the afternoon, he received a call from Anatoly, who informed him that there had been no news and Gregor had gone to ground. He asked Jussi if he wouldn't mind spending the next day at the Police Station to fill in some gaps and add valuable information. Jussi agreed, and after checking with his superior, he was booked on the plane to Helsinki the following evening.

♦ ♦ ♦

Jussi's final day in Russia dragged, mainly being spent on reports and answering questions from the Russian police. Anatoly dropped by and joined him for lunch, thanking him for his help and extending his hospitality anytime that Jussi might find himself back in Russia.

"Perhaps next time, you will not disappear so quickly!" he laughed, shaking hands with Jussi.

♦ ♦ ♦

It was with considerable relief that Jussi boarded the plane that evening. He closed his eyes and sighed with satisfaction when the plane took off and headed towards Helsinki.

"I'm going home at last!" he mouthed to himself.

DODGING BULLETS

Jussi awoke. For the first time in over a week, he was home. He looked up at the ceiling of his apartment, with the sun streaming in through the window, eyeing the thin white curtains once more.

It was early, just before 6 am, but he was just happy to be back home. He looked out of the window into the courtyard and nodded, appreciating where he lived. He wasn't due at the station until later that morning, so he took the opportunity to relax a little. He showered, dressed casually and wandered over to a café he enjoyed visiting. He ordered their signature full breakfast at the bar and took a seat by the window overlooking the square. He was still without a smartphone, so he took one of the newspapers from the stand and sat back to read the latest news.

A large cappuccino arrived from a young waitress, and Jussi flashed her a big smile. The coffee was excellent, as was the large plate of food that came soon after, containing orange juice, ham, eggs, toast and a croissant.

Jussi happily wiled away an hour over his breakfast and delighted in doing something so simple and enjoyable. It turned his thoughts away from the events of the past week.

He idly leafed through the newspaper and came across the property page. He stopped for a moment as a thought suddenly crossed his mind.

What about the building that Gregor bought here in Helsinki? he thought.

As it was unlikely that anyone was following up on this yet, he decided to pay it a visit in case there might be any activity inside, or a clue to its owner's whereabouts. He doubted it, but his curious mind couldn't help wanting to find out for himself. After all, it was nearby, and he could check it now and be one step ahead when he made an appearance at the station.

If he had his phone, he could check where it was and walk there but having lost not one but two phones in the last days; Jussi had decided that he would arrange a proper one later at the station. Therefore, he decided to navigate his way in the traditional style. He wandered over to the bar and smiled at the waitress once more. She was happy to give him directions, and he added a few notes onto the newspaper and thanked her. While doing so, he realised the paper he was writing on belonged to the café, apologised and offered to pay, but she gestured for him to keep it.

He made off across the square and over the main road, towards the address in question. With the sun on his face, it took him about fifteen minutes, while walking briskly. It was a stroll he would have been happy to do on a day like this, especially as he hadn't had much exercise recently.

Jussi arrived at the building and surveyed it with interest: it had an attractive facade. It was an older one that had been renovated and spruced up with a coat of white paint. He surveyed the heavy wooden door, which wouldn't have looked out of place on a castle. It was closed and locked. There was a line of brass call buttons on the wall, and he noted that only one of them seemed to be labelled and occupied. The sign read: Carlton Enterprises Oy.

Well, that could be anything, he thought. It could be

a company renting the space, or it could be the criminal organisation itself.

He thought for a moment and pressed the button, thinking of a cover story. A few seconds later, a female voice spoke through the speaker, impatiently and hurried.

"Hello, who is it?" the voice inquired in English, with a Russian accent.

"Hello, my name is Pekka Holmqvist. I'm a local handyman, and I'm checking to see if any small jobs need doing in the area."

"What? No, we don't have any need for that, goodbye."

Then, the voice returned.

"Sorry, what kind of things do you do? We have some cabinets and pictures that need hanging. Is that something you could do cheaply?"

"Oh yes, you'll find my rates are very reasonable," Jussi replied.

"Come on up then. Top floor. Ring the bell when you get here."

A buzzer sounded, and he pushed the door: it opened. Having got this far, Jussi was happy to chance his luck again. If he could find out anything useful, it could be worth hanging a few pictures.

He took the small lift to the top floor and rang the bell at the main entrance. There were a few doors leading off the landing but only one of them opened. It took Jussi a bit by surprise with the speed and force by which it was opened from the other side.

In the doorway stood an attractive, tall woman, about his age, tastefully and expensively dressed, in blue.

Jussi smiled and tried to look like a tradesperson. His clothes were casual, but he suddenly realised that he had no tools.

"Hello, where are your tools?" she asked, looking him up and down.

"Ah."

Jussi thought quickly.

"I was just in the area, doing a little advertising."

"Well, that's okay, we still have some of the decorators' tools back there. They only did half of the inside and then disappeared. Can you believe it? Maybe you can finish their job if they don't return?"

"I'd be happy to do that, but for now perhaps, just the pictures," Jussi suggested.

"Well, whatever the case, we need to get the office ready as quickly as possible. Our boss is coming to visit, and everything must be ready," she explained.

The lady took Jussi through a recently repainted office, renovated as far as some unused offices at the end. After the lobby, there was one large room and several smaller ones. Jussi didn't see anyone else and couldn't help wondering who her boss was and if it could even be Gregor.

Some rooms had their doors open and contained modern furniture with computers and printers lying around. It was obviously a work in progress. Jussi was shown to the back office, where some tools and a large toolbox lay on the floor.

The woman gestured to some pictures lying on the floor and explained how they should be hung, equally spaced, down the corridor. She told him when he had finished, he should find her, and she would show him where to put the others. With that, she disappeared.

Taking a drill and some parts, Jussi took the first picture. They were original watercolours and seemed quite old, with ornate guilt frames. He thought they looked a little out of place at first but decided they looked rather good after hanging them. The overall effect was of an art gallery.

After thirty minutes, he completed his task and tidied the floor. Afterwhich, he went to find the woman: currently still nameless. As he did so, he realised this was a perfect moment to snoop around. After all, he wasn't to know where she was, and he could now legitimately wander around at his leisure.

The woman didn't seem to be anywhere as he checked each office. While moving around the space, though, he became aware of the security cameras in every corner of the corridor and foyer. He made a conscious effort to behave as naturally as possible from that point onwards.

Jussi entered the large office set out like a conference room, with a long meeting table and desk at one end. He remembered this as being in the old-fashioned Russian style: an important manager would sit at the large desk, and his minions would line up at the table in front of it. In this case, the wood was not old-fashioned; it was light coloured and modern. There were no cameras in this room, so he casually looked at some papers left lying around. He didn't find anything apart from invoices or delivery notes, though, it seemed that business had not yet commenced.

Jussi heard voices outside and made himself look busy by picking up a painting and placing it against a wall. The doors opened, and the woman returned. Behind her, two men walked in. Jussi immediately recognised one of the men, and he realised it was Jussi with the same speed.

"Well, what a coincidence," said Gregor, as his assistant removed a pistol from his jacket and levelled it at Jussi. "Please sit down, Jussi. I imagine that painting must be getting rather heavy."

Gregor's assistant came across the room and sat Jussi down by his shoulder, moving behind him, the gun levelled at his head. The woman, Natalja, was horrified, having just realised that she had invited the police into the new headquarters of their criminal organisation, and her boss had just walked in on him. Jussi was equally shocked - the appearance of Gregor confirmed his involvement in this building.

How did he get out of Russia? Jussi wondered.

He realised that someone as wealthy as Gregor probably had connections everywhere, and his money could buy many favours.

"You've cost me a great deal of money and trouble, Jussi. I was quite reasonable when I warned you to stay out of my affairs."

"You tried to frame me for murder and had my associate from Latvia killed, Jussi said," his voice filled with menace. "I wouldn't call that reasonable."

"You need to remember what I say, Jussi. I don't do these things, but my associates must do what they must in order to protect our organisation. Now, it seems we must start all over again, and thanks to you, I may never be able to return to Russia under my name. You've already met my colleague Natalja who has spent a lot of time and effort trying to sort out the mess you've caused, both in Latvia and Finland."

Natalja looked as if she could happily pull the trigger to shoot Jussi herself. She wasn't looking forward to the conversation that would take place with Gregor about her new handyman. Jussi sat quietly and listened, as his mind focused on any possible way out of the situation.

"Ivan," he said to his assistant. It's Jussi, who almost put all of us in prison, or under the earth for that matter. Please take him somewhere and kill him. Oh, I'm sorry, Jussi, I've changed my management style recently, thanks to you."

"My station knows where I am, and they have this address. Why don't you just tie me up and leave? You could get away without any more charges. If you kill me, you'll have every agency in Finland looking for you."

"Really? I'm not convinced," spat Gregor. "I'm not going to become some fugitive on the run. This office is where I will resurrect my whole organisation. We have already got Latvia up and running, and my friends in Russia will handle everything there. No, it's you, Jussi, who will leave but not how you might choose. Natalja, go with Ivan and deal with this. There are plenty of forests in Finland. Go and plant him in one.

Gregor turned away.

"Now, if everyone will excuse me, I have work to do."

"I'm not going anywhere with you," said Jussi stubbornly.

"Oh yes, you are. If there are any problems along the way, then I will visit your girlfriend. Selma, isn't it?" Gregor asked.

Jussi fell silent. He had no idea that they had investigated his life and couldn't risk anything happening to Selma.

Ivan lifted and marched him towards the door. He felt the gun barrel digging into his back. They walked out of the office and took the old lift down to the ground floor. Jussi's mind was racing as he thought of all possible exits: there didn't seem to be any.

At the bottom of the stairs, they turned him towards a door that swung open, revealing concrete steps leading downwards in a spiral. Jussi guessed it might lead to a small carpark. Knowing this path would lead to certain death sooner or later, he decided to act there and then, when his captors would least expect it.

Suddenly, he dropped to the floor and, as he did so, grabbed Ivan's leg and pulled him down. A muffled shot rang out as he tumbled down the stairs, audibly cracking his head on the concrete as he did so.

At that point, Natalja pulled out a pistol herself. Jussi hadn't considered that she would have a gun. She levelled it at him, so he rolled over the railing, landing roughly and painfully on the ground. Seeing the gun pointing down above him, he grabbed at it. As Natalja fired over the side, a bullet hit the concrete. Jussi dived under the stairs and grazed his head in the process. He saw Ivan's gun lying on the ground, grabbed it and turned, firing one round after another. He heard a scream and footsteps as she ran back up the stairs.

Jussi orientated himself and stood up. He hadn't realised how hard he'd fallen but did so at that moment: his head ached, and a shooting pain surged through his thigh into the small of his back. He staggered around the corner and noted that Ivan was either dead or out cold; either way, he wasn't moving.

Jussi made his way up the stairs, lurching from one side to another. As he opened the door, a shot struck the door. Jussi kicked it and fired two shots at Natalja as she stood there, ready to fire again - but she fell to the ground.

All the guns were silent now, but Jussi had no idea if Gregor had heard the sound of the shots. He got into the lift and pressed the button to the top floor.

As Jussi rose upwards, he scanned the staircase for movement. Seeing nothing, he arrived at the door, kicked it and walked in without ceremony. He spun around with his gun aimed but saw nothing. He painfully moved a large cabinet across the door with his back and started to move through the offices. It took him some minutes to discover that there was no-one there.

Then, a thought hit him, *Selma*.

Jussi ran back to the main door and somehow pulled the cabinet away. He sailed down the stairs, half staggering and half balancing on the railing and stepped out into the street. He staggered out with blood across his face, holding a gun.

A few pedestrians were walking around, who immediately scattered at the sight of Jussi. As he looked around the street, he returned to the building and scrambled down to the carpark.

Of course, they had a car and would have car keys, Jussi thought.

He checked and found a key in the motionless Ivan's pocket and pressed the button: a car blipped, and its lights flashed on. He searched the other jacket pocket and found a mobile phone, clambered into the saloon and started the car.

The garage door opened automatically as he drove upwards, setting off towards Selma's apartment. He punched the phone with his fingers and rang what he thought might be her number.

"Please be there or be somewhere safe," he muttered to himself.

Miraculously, it was the correct number, and Selma answered after three rings.

"Selma, where are you?" he asked.

"I'm at home. I have a day off today, and if you had called me, maybe we could have met up?"

"Please do as I say. Lock everything, put something against the door and don't go out. I'll be there in ten minutes. You're in danger, Selma. Whatever you do, don't answer the door!"

Selma sensed the urgency in his voice and immediately went to lock the door and drop the chain. She sat down with her phone in her hand, hoping the next knock on the door would belong to

Jussi.

◆ ◆ ◆

Gregor sat in the taxi as it made its way towards Selma's apartment. He was seething with anger. Both Natalja and his bodyguard were probably dead, and he was on the run again, this time in Finland. He tried calling some of his associates, and there was either a dead tone, an answerphone, or someone else answered the phone. Clearly, the Russian police had been hard at work attacking the Vipers over the past 24 hours.

As they drove through Helsinki, he mapped out his plan. He would kidnap Selma and use her as a bargaining chip for as long as necessary. Then, he would get over the border along the eastern side, with the help of some friends inside the Russian police. After that, he would hide out in his countryside dacha, which he was convinced nobody knew the whereabouts of. The cottage had a laptop, phone, money, weapons and everything he would need to hide. The organisation would need to take second place for a while. Now, it was all about survival.

◆ ◆ ◆

Jussi accelerated as he moved out of the traffic and found an open road. A speed camera flashed as he powered through; he would explain that one later. He estimated it would take him another ten minutes to reach Selma. He planned that they would leave the apartment and get far away. Remembering Russia, he didn't want to risk having police protection at the apartment. He didn't know what might be coming his way, so decided to put as much distance as possible between him and Gregor. He would drive to Rauma with Selma.

As he drove, he punched in the station number and made it through to Tapio after a couple of transfers. He explained what was happening and gave him Selma's address.

At the station, Tapio dashed out from his desk and rustled up some help. The group dived into the elevator to the carpark and took two cars from the selection lined up in front of them.

Tapio barked out orders on the telephone as they drove, mobilising multiple police cars to head towards Selma's address.

◆ ◆ ◆

After what seemed like an age, Jussi pulled into the car park, left the vehicle, and ran to the apartment block entrance. His eyes darted around, looking for a sign of Gregor or some other threat, but he didn't see any. He rang the bell, and Selma answered.

"Selma, it's me, Jussi. Open the door."

Recognising his voice, Selma buzzed him in and waited behind the locked door. Hearing his voice outside the door, she opened it with the chain on and was relieved to see his face.

"What the hell is going on?" she asked.

"Sorry, no time to explain. Get your car keys and let's go."

A confused Selma grabbed her handbag and went with Jussi as he took her by the arm.

"Your car?" he asked.

"It's in the garage; here are the keys," she answered, handing them to him.

Jussi took the keys, and they dived into the car. He drove the short way to the entrance, and the automatic door slowly opened at his approach. He counted the seconds for it to open, enough to go through. Seeing nobody in front of him, he pressed the accelerator hard, speeding out of the apartment block across the small carpark. He saw a familiar figure standing in front of him as he did so.

"Down!" yelled Jussi.

Selma complied.

Jussi swerved away, as glass shattered with the force of bullets from Gregor's gun as he shot into the car multiple times. Luckily, Jussi managed to out-manoeuvre the attack and they sped away towards the main road that would take them towards the city of Turku and onwards to Rauma and safety.

CLOSE SHAVE

Jussi paid little attention to speed limits on his way to Rauma and cut the journey down to less than two and a half hours, wanting to get Selma as far away as possible.

He called Tapio along the way.

"Tapsa, it's Jussi."

"Jussi, how are you and Selma? Where are you?"

Jussi explained what had happened and informed Tapio of his plan.

"I'm heading towards Rauma. We'll hide out there for a few days until Gregor gets captured and this whole thing goes away."

"Okay, that's a good decision. Half the police force of Helsinki is out looking for Gregor at the moment, so I'm sure we'll find him soon enough. I'll let the station in Rauma know you're there. Get some sleep, and I'll call you tomorrow morning."

Jussi and Selma talked for some time, with Jussi narrating the story, Selma asking questions, and Jussi filling in the answers he could.

After an hour and a half of discussion, they were tired, and the conversation dried up. It was dark when they finally arrived.

Despite the circumstances, Jussi smiled when he turned into the familiar old town of Rauma and rounded the tight corner into his small yard. He parked next to his jeep and woke Selma, who had been asleep for the past hour.

"Wakey, wakey."

Jussi smiled as Selma stretched and yawned. He opened the door, and they went into the house.

Both being exhausted, they went straight to bed. However, Jussi lay awake thinking about the events of the past 24 hours, but soon succumbed to sleep himself.

◆ ◆ ◆

The following day, Jussi opened his eyes to find Selma sitting next to him on the bed with two mugs of coffee.

"I thought you might need one of these?" she smiled.

"Nevermore than this morning," he answered, gratefully accepting the mug from her.

Then he put his mug down, took her's and kissed her, holding her close for some time. He hadn't spent much time with her recently and was very grateful that she was close to him now.

"So, is your job always this dangerous? Do all of your girlfriends have to go through this?" she asked.

Jussi briefly thought about his previous experiences and answered.

"Not always, just the interesting ones", he said with a smile.

"Well, let's hope there are no repeat performances, Jussi. If we stay together as a couple, I'm not sure how much of this excitement I can take."

Jussi smiled again, feeling reassured by her words. He looked into her eyes.

"Come on," he said. "I'm going to take you to my favourite

places today."

"Maybe we could go shopping too," she smiled. "I didn't bring any spare clothes."

"Yes, of course."

He suddenly remembered he was at home, but Selma only had the clothes she stood up in. She made a call to her optical store and arranged for her appointments to be suspended for a few days, while Jussi called the station in Rauma and arranged to meet his old colleagues on the following day and update them on recent events. He also spoke to both Tapio and Pekka, who told him to take the day off with Selma.

They spent the rest of the morning gently wandering around the old town, as Jussi still felt fragile from his minor injuries. They did some shopping for Selma, and she bought clothes for a few days. Afterwards, they visited his favourite café, ordering a large pulla with each cappuccino. Jussi felt happy to be home. Helsinki had its appeal, but he was more than happy to return for a spell.

As they sat idly chatting, he started to wonder if he had experienced enough excitement for now and perhaps, he was more suited to the gentler pace of Rauma. At least nobody had tried to kill him here.

"A penny for your thoughts?" Selma asked, moving into his gaze.

"I was just wondering if I should come back here, sooner rather than later," he said.

"Well, it's a beautiful place, Jussi. It's a lot quieter than Helsinki, though. Of course, if you had some company here....?" her voice trailed off.

Jussi smiled at her.

"Do you mean you would like to come to Rauma?" he asked.

"I've enjoyed Helsinki, but I've been thinking about living in a smaller place, closer to nature and trying a different lifestyle for a while."

They chatted casually about the idea. The more they spoke, the more Jussi found himself attracted to it, especially with Selma.

After the conversation, they returned to the apartment, and it wasn't long before they moved to the bedroom.

◆ ◆ ◆

When Jussi awoke, he was hungry. He quietly got out of bed and put on a t-shirt and shorts. Then, he slipped out of the bedroom, into the kitchen. He checked the fridge and cupboards and remembered there was no food in the house - he hadn't been here in a long time. He recalled a leaflet on top of a pile of mail that his neighbour had left him about a new Italian restaurant with a delivery service. He found it and called to order a couple of pizzas. It was early, and the restaurant said they would be ready quickly, so he agreed to collect them in thirty minutes. Next, he checked on Selma, who was fast asleep, so he wrote a short note and left it on the kitchen counter.

It was still warm, and Jussi put on a pair of sandals and walked a couple of streets to the restaurant. The smell was fantastic, and he received the pizzas gratefully and paid. He also bought a couple of cold beers and tucked them under his arm. Smelling the pizzas, he walked back, happy with his decision. He would certainly appreciate this place if he moved back to Rauma. He opened the door and called Selma as he kicked off his sandals and placed the pizzas on the counter. He opened the drawer to find a bottle opener, and as he did so, he looked up and found himself staring down the barrel of a gun.

"Did you think you could just disappear after what you did to me?" questioned Gregor menacingly, thrusting the pistol in his direction.

Jussi mouth had dropped open, and he was struck dumb for a moment. When he recovered, he scanned the room to check on Selma - he didn't see her.

"Are you looking for your girlfriend?"

"Where is she?" Jussi growled.

A gun in his face wasn't going to stop his anger this time.

"She's still sleeping, Jussi. She woke up and came in here for a drink of water, read your note and then went back to sleep. I was sitting here the whole time. You must have tired her out today, so I'm going to leave her sleeping. Don't worry; my fight is not with her. I've arranged my escape and don't need her anymore. I certainly don't need you anymore, Jussi. You've interfered with my plans for the final time. Close your eyes and prepare to die."

Jussi thought quickly but couldn't think of any more options. He was at least happy that nothing would happen to Selma. He stared back at Gregor with hate in his eyes.

"They'll find you, Gregor, and you'll never see the outside of a prison cell again."

"I don't think so, Jussi. Some have tried before; however, here I am. I have plenty left to do in my life. You, on the other hand, do not."

Jussi held his breath, and Gregor turned him around to face the wall. There was nothing he could do now.

Gregor began to squeeze the trigger, and Jussi stood and waited for the bullet. Then, something entirely unexpected happened.

❖ ❖ ❖

Selma awoke. She had heard Jussi's entry to the kitchen and slowly rose from the bed.

She was sitting on the bed, putting on her underwear, when she heard voices. She slowly moved towards the door and saw the back of someone talking to Jussi; he had a gun in his hand and was pointing it at him. Selma wasn't a courageous girl, but with Jussi threatened, she found something within herself at that moment.

She quietly moved forwards in her bare feet. Without making a sound and unknown to neither Gregor nor Jussi - she lifted a beer bottle and continued to move silently towards them.

As Gregor found the trigger, Selma brought the bottle down on his head with so much force that it not only knocked him to the floor but exploded the bottle. There was absolute chaos for a moment as the beer exploded and frothed everywhere.

Jussi turned around, hearing the sound but feeling no bullet. Then he saw Selma. She was standing in her underwear, drenched from head to toe, with Gregor lying on the floor. Perhaps it was relief or the situation that had just played out before them that they both looked at each other and laughed.

Jussi dropped to one knee and found Gregor was out cold, as he'd hit his head on the floor, and so grabbed the gun and moved away, taking Selma's arm. He took the phone from his pocket and called the police station.

They both stood in silence until reinforcements arrived. With some amazement, Jussi's police colleagues filed into the apartment. They shook their head as they beheld the sight. His old partner Harri took a step towards him and shook his hand.

Selma suddenly became embarrassed, standing in revealing

underwear, covered in beer. The story was to become a legend at the station, which Harri would remind Jussi of, on a regular basis.

IN RAUMA

In Rauma, the meetings and conference calls over the following days kept Jussi busy, but he was delighted to return to Selma each evening.

Gregor was still in hospital and would undoubtedly spend the rest of his life in a high-security Russian jail. His organisation had, by now, disintegrated, with the remaining parts grasped by ambitious colleagues for themselves.

After the publicity faded away, Selma found herself back at work in Helsinki, dealing with the backlog of appointments that had built up in her absence.

Jussi found himself back at the station in Helsinki. The amount of paperwork to be completed about the case was substantial due to the scale of Gregor's organisation.

◆ ◆ ◆

One evening, Jussi and Selma found themselves back at the same sushi restaurant where they had initially met. They ordered the same food and drank the same excellent bottle of wine. They also laughed a lot and talked about a possible future together.

The conversation continued over the following days, and they found themselves wanting to be together as much as possible. Jussi had talked speculatively with his superiors in Rauma and Helsinki, and a detective position in Rauma was subsequently made available. This role was to be combined with a development opportunity that would take him towards a Detective Sergeant position over the following five years.

Selma also had conversations with prospective optical stores. After a few telephone calls, she found one in Rauma that would be more than happy to welcome someone of her experience. She could start as soon as she liked.

During another evening, over Jussi's homemade Spaghetti Bolognese and a bottle of Amarone, they agreed to their plan.

They spent the following month working out their respective notice periods at their places of work and arranged to move at the end of summer. Selma put her apartment up for rent and organised her possessions to be moved to Jussi's apartment in Rauma, which went smoothly.

◆ ◆ ◆

"How does it feel to be back in Rauma, Jussi?" Pekka asked at a small gathering in a local restaurant, arranged to welcome him back.

"It's great," said Jussi. It'll be a change of pace from Helsinki, but I'm enjoying it."

"Are you sure, Jussi?" remarked Harri.

"Oh yes, and you never know, Harri. Remember 'The Paintings of Rauma' case? I'm also looking forward to living in the old town again, visiting my favourite places, watching ice hockey, kayaking, photography, and spending time with Selma. Oh, and not getting threatened or shot at will be nice too!"

Everyone laughed. The whole police force in Rauma was pleased to see Jussi back. It had only been half a year, but Jussi had already proved his worth many times.

❖ ❖ ❖

Over the following weeks, the couple happily settled into a routine.

After an invitation from Jussi's Uncle, they arranged a weekend at his cabin. This time, it was just the two of them. It was well-stocked, and they were delighted to discover two kayaks in the boat-house.

One fine evening, during the last summer days, they set out from the dock, gliding across the perfectly still water, with the sun slowly sinking. As they skimmed through the water together, they talked.

"It's so beautiful here," Selma commented as they gently paddled towards the lake's centre.

"Yes, it's a nice change. I remember the last time I paddled in a kayak. It's a bit different here, compared to the waves of Helsinki," replied Jussi, with a wide grin on his face.

The End

ABOUT THE AUTHOR

John Swallow

I am originally from Yorkshire, England and have been fortunate to have also lived in countries as diverse as Scotland, Argentina, Latvia and now Finland.

I enjoy writing crime adventures and about the supernatural. The common factor in my stories is that they are usually based in Finland and often in my adopted home town of Rauma.

Thank you for reading my book. If you wish, you can follow my writing at: https://raumastories.blogspot.com

And if you a few moments to spare, a short review would be greatly appreciated on Amazon or Goodreads. Thank you!

I hope you enjoyed reading this novel as much as I enjoyed writing it!

THE JUSSI ALONEN DETECTIVE ADVENTURES

Jussi Alonen is a Police Officer, based in Rauma, Finland. His career takes him towards his ambition to be a detective and beyond.

From being based in Rauma and then Helsinki, his journey takes him on a series of exciting adventures to many different countries. Follow Jussi across Finland, Sweden, Singapore, Latvia, Russia and even Cuba!.

His challenges include theft, murder and organised crime. In addition, his romantic interludes give him just as much cause to struggle.

Follow Jussi's adventures in: The Paintings of Rauma, The Waves of Helsinki and now, The Heat of Havana and join Jussi Alonen for a taste of Finland's Nordic Noir.

The Paintings Of Rauma

The Paintings of Rauma takes the reader to Finland for a thrilling crime adventure. The story is based in the beautiful coastal city of Rauma and takes Jussi, a local police officer, on a journey to investigate connected crimes across Finland, Sweden and Singapore.

This Nordic Noir mystery begins with a minor incident that sets in motion a chain of events involving theft, murder, passion and hidden treasure.

Jussi is a local Police Officer whose life is turned upside down when someone from the past comes back into his life. A gang of criminals make their way around Finland, wreaking havoc in search of great wealth. Treasure from the past is found and millions are made and then lost.

Jussi discovers there is more to police work in Rauma than he could ever imagine.

The Waves Of Helsinki

The Waves of Helsinki takes the reader back to Finland for a thrilling new crime adventure. This time, the story is based in Helsinki, the spectacular capital city of Finland.

Jussi Alonen is now training to be a detective and becomes involved in an intriguing investigation which quickly escalates.

This Nordic Noir mystery begins with some apparently small thefts, which if not stopped, will escalate to the spread of major organised crime.

Jussi's career is heading towards his ambition of being a fully-fledged detective, that's if he can survive the events in Helsinki, Latvia, Russia and his home town of Rauma.

Theft and murder on the high seas, combined with a new romance, will challenge Jussi more than he ever thought possible.

The Heat Of Havana

The Heat of Havana finds Detective Jussi Alonen settled down in Rauma once again. However, little does he know that a thrilling new adventure awaits him, one which will not only reconnect him with an old flame but also result in his involvement with international crime once again.

Smuggling high-quality Cuban cigars to wealthy Eastern Europeans is a lucrative business. However, when a problem arises, Jussi's old friend Heli finds herself in the wrong place at the wrong time and he unexpectedly finds himself in Havana. Can he save her and return to his life as a detective in Finland?

This Nordic Noir mystery gradually evolves into high-octane action as Jussi's new nemesis follows him from Cuba to Finland, with both bent on revenge, in this gripping new story.

Cigars, mojitos and rumba turn into kidnapping, smuggling and murder, immersing Jussi in his most exciting adventure yet!

Printed in Great Britain
by Amazon